THE LOST ART OF SINKING

Naomi Booth grew up in West Yorkshire. She read English at the University of Cambridge and completed a PhD in Creative and Critical Writing at the University of Sussex. Her short fiction has been published as part of Myriad Editions' Quick Fictions series and her first novella was shortlisted for the MMU Novella award in 2014. Her critical work has been published in *New Formations* and *Textual Practice*, and she is currently working on a monograph about swooning. Naomi lives in York and is a Lecturer in Literature and Creative Writing.

The Lost Art of Sinking

Naomi Booth

Penned in the Margins

LONDON

PUBLISHED BY PENNED IN THE MARGINS
Toynbee Studios, 28 Commercial Street, London E1 6AB
www.pennedinthemargins.co.uk

The right of Naomi Booth to be identified as the author of this work has been asserted by her in accordance with Section 77 of the Copyright, Designs and Patent Act 1988.

First published 2014

Printed in the United Kingdom by Berforts Information Press Ltd.

ISBN
978-1-908058-29-4

ACKNOWLEDGEMENTS

I would like to thank the following people for their generous friendship, brilliant advice and patient reading of this book at its various madcap stages: Toby Smart, Nicholas Royle, Kate Murray-Browne, Helen Jukes, Laura Joyce, Tom Houlton, Dulcie Few, Michael Fake, Kieran Devaney, Tom Chivers and Tom Bunstead. My parents, Jane and Ian Booth, have supported me in myriad ways, for which I am immensely grateful. I would also like to thank the Arts and Humanities Research Council for their sponsorship during the time that this work was written.

for Michael Fake

The Lost Art
of Sinking

I
De-oxygenation

I suppose you could call it a talent. A gift, perhaps. Except that I had to work at it. It didn't come straight away. The first time I tried it, I was thirteen years-old. I'd cut my teeth on mother grief, so I wanted it more than any of the others. We all filed into the hall together, the girls of 2B, in our burgundy skirts and uncooperative cardigans, pumps scuffing against the parquet. The secret crackled silently along the line of us. As we moved into place, we flickered our eyes towards one another, already aware of a slight shortness of breath: the effect of anticipation. Once the whole school was assembled, Mr Tweedle, perched on the stage above us, began his monologue: "Today's thought comes from Jalal ad-Din Muhammad Rumi." His voice rose and fell away, with a mystic's cadence. "The great Persian poet and theologian. This is what he says to us: 'Yesterday I was clever, so I wanted to change the world. Today I am wise, so I am changing myself'."

As Mr Tweedle expounded the history of the Sultanate of Rum and the Seljuq dynasty, we girls of 2B covertly scrutinised one another, to check that no one was starting before time. We all made a show of breathing as normally as possible — shoulders back, chests forward — and some of us furrowed our brows in a way that suggested a zero-tolerance approach to cheating. When the organ started up, the pages of hymn books rustled towards 'Blessed Assurance'. It was time: the game was afoot. Whilst seeming to sing, we began to make our breath as quick and shallow as possible. I imagine we must have looked like tiny dogs, our heads bobbing as we panted between each word. We kept this up until the very last verse, at which point each of us held our breath for as long as possible. The boys around us knew that something strange was going on — we created a soft shushing sound, whipped up by the collective hyperventilation — but couldn't be sure quite what. Miss Briscoe stood at the side, anxiously surveying the line of us. Three of her girls had gone down in the previous week; she couldn't understand it. She'd given us all a long talk on the importance of a substantial breakfast.

But Leanne Hrymoc had got to us first. At a sleepover the weekend before, she had introduced the decision-makers of 2B to the Fainting Game. I wasn't included, but I got to hear about it soon enough.

"My cousin taught me. She's 16 and she's shagging that policeman," Leanne had said to the others. "It makes you go all rushy. You feel like you're falling into a dream."

"Oh, I've heard of it. The *Dying Game*," Laura Murgatroyd had cut in. "I heard some girl in Barnsley killed herself doing it."

"Yeah, my sister calls it Indian Headrush," Anna McAvoy added. "You can *totally* die from it."

They had all agreed. We would secretly play the Fainting Game every day in assembly the following week. The winner would be the girl who passed out the most times. Or, in the case of a tie, whoever passed out in the most dramatic way. If anyone died, they scored an automatic win. If more than one person died, the winner was the girl who died in the coolest way. No starving, no faking: it had to be real.

So I stood in line, my eyes beginning to glaze with the effort of concentration. I didn't really know what I was doing, back then. I dragged the air through my mouth in desperate, covert rushes; I could feel it roughing up the back of my throat. And as the hymn reached the final verse I gulped in everything I could. I quickly scanned along the line, searching for the girls who might be teetering. Laura, at my right-hand side, looked perfectly serene: eyes closed, mouth sealed. But she hadn't gone down yet either. Anna was looking more likely; her cheeks were flushed and her right hand had begun to flutter. I closed my eyes for extra disorientation. I tried to force my weight forwards, into the balls of my feet, to encourage disequilibrium. I let my head fall back slightly. And then I think it *almost* happened: the darkness behind my eyes began to swim into a kind of green. I tried to sink into it, to let my brain soften. But I was still a novice. My thoughts refused to blur. I could feel my brain ticking with concentration, all nerves and electricity. I could still follow the words of the hymnal; I could call to mind my lessons for that morning. And then I heard a scuffle down the line to my left. I opened my eyes, and let go of my breath. A clearing had formed around Anna, who was curled on her side on the hall floor, with one arm around her head. Second time this week. She had fallen, audaciously, into the lead.

After school that day, I went back to Laura's house. The Murgatroyds lived in an enormous blackened vicarage in the bottom of the valley, next to the church. It was the sort of house we used to tell stories about when we were younger; everyone was a little bit scared of it. But I used to visit whenever I could. Really old people lived on the upper two floors, looked after by Laura's mother. I suppose it was some sort of small private care home, but it seemed like a far more mysterious and macabre arrangement back then. As we sat in Laura's bedroom, the calls of an old woman sirened in, again and again, even when we turned the music up. Sometimes the woman screamed for a full five seconds. From Laura's bedroom window, I could see the old headstones in the churchyard, haphazard and laced with lichen. I rested my head against the glass as Laura practised her dance moves.

"What's wrong with you?" Laura shouted at me, jerking her way through her bogle finale. Laura was always singing along to ragga tracks in her patchy West Yorkshire patois. She came to a breathless stop on the bed. "Is it your mum, Esther?" Laura asked, lying down beside me, taking my hand and stroking it. "Are you thinking of your mum?" she asked again, with the salacious solicitude all the girls had adopted since my mother died. Suddenly, everyone had wanted to be my best friend, to lead me into the girls' loos to share claustrophobic confidences about my grief.

"I'm thinking about the game." I withdrew my hand. "I just want to know what it's like."

Anna McAvoy had spent a long time at break euphorically filling us non-swooners in on what we were missing. She saw things, she said, before she went down. Strange and beautiful shapes; and they were *that* beautiful, they were what *made* her go. They were shapes she recognised, but didn't recognise. Like things returning; like ghosts, or something. It was like falling into a different world, she said. Leanne Hrymoc had laughed and said she was touched. But I thought it sounded like the most wonderful thing and I hoarded that possibility inside myself.

"I just want to see it. I want to feel it, like Anna did."

Laura thought for a while. "You *really* want to get out of your head? Off your face?"

"I suppose. If that's what it is…" I said.

"You know, there are other ways to do it."

"Yeah?"

"Like what my brother and his mates do on a weekend.

Like gak."

"Gak?"

"You know." Laura bit her lip with excitement.

I think I half-knew I was being duped, but I didn't care that much. I was willing to try almost anything. Laura said she had some arrangements to make. She disappeared for a couple of minutes, and then she came back for me. I followed her down to the cellar, where enormous washing machines sat on top of one another and there were two industrial dryers, to manage the old people's laundry. Grey flannel bedding was hung out at one end of the room and there was an old stone wash-sink in the middle, without any taps. We were below ground level here and one oblong window showed us the line of the churchyard grass above our heads. I remember the subterranean cold and how it seemed to seep inwards and upwards through the walls and floor. I began to think laterally, to imagine directly outwards through the earth of the churchyard, towards my mother. And then an image flashed into my head: a coffin full of hair. It was that thing people always say about dead bodies and the hair keeping on growing; I thought of my mother cocooned in her own prodigious hair.

"Let's get on with it," I said.

"So," Laura said, "here it is. The *stuff*." There were two thick, grainy lines of white powder poured out in parallel on the stone sink. It made me think of quicklime.

"So what do we do?"

"We get down like this." Laura bent over towards the surface, so that her nose was hovering over the powder crystals. She nipped one nostril closed with her first finger and mimed hoovering down the line. "And then you suck it up like that. You first!" Laura stepped back, the magnanimous host.

"Ok." I stepped up. I shut down one side of my nose and sniffed up as hard as I could. I could feel the powder filling up the bottom of my nostril cavity, like a liquid. And then I could feel a sharp sting, burning up my sinuses.

"Ow," I squawked. "Ow, ow, ow."

"Does it not feel ... good?" Laura asked.

"It feels ... like it's burning." I was having to move from one foot to the other now, and fanning my hands at either side of my nose. "Is it supposed to feel like this?"

Laura watched me for a few moments with a strange expression on her face. "To be honest, Ettie, I thought I'd try you on soap powder first. Just to see if you could handle it. It's all chemicals, right?" She swept her fat line of Daz down the plughole. "I think I'll give it a miss."

"Oh god," I said. "I can feel it at the back of my throat. It's disgusting."

"So, maybe we need to, maybe, wash it out?"

We ran up to the bathroom and Laura held my hair, while I splashed water into my nose and mouth. I gargled again and again, spitting out soap clouds, but my tongue kept on lathering.

Later, when it started to get dark, Mrs Murgatroyd said that my Dad would be worrying, that I should be going home. So I wound my way back along the canal path. I knew my Dad would still be at work and that the house would be empty. So I slowed down, dawdling despite the cold. I lent against the canal wall; it was so enormous, the wall, stones like boulders, that it seemed to hold back the banked-up earth of the whole valley, which rose above it. I looked into the black water, rippling from the edge where a coot was bedding down. I stared up to the horizon, the top of the other side of the valley where the last line of light was cracking over the hills. If I stayed much longer, I knew the canal path would be pitch dark and I'd have to feel my way home along the wall. I suppose it was a sort of intuition. The coming dark made it seem possible. So I started practising my breathing. I shuddered the air through my body as violently as possible. My throat was even more raw now and I could follow the circles that the air was making through me by its sting. As the last light sank below the horizon, I locked my breath inside my body. Everything went dark. Tiny flittering stars started to appear beyond my eyes. The ground began to swim. I could feel everything in my body swoop suddenly downwards. And I stumbled back, into the dark, against the wall. I was only out for a moment, but it was a start.

II

Primal Scenes

I should explain about my mother. I grew up in a house at the edge of the Todmorden canal: a squat lock-keeper's cottage, blasted back to the colour of sand. It had ridiculous gates, which my father had painted gold. Despite his gaudy touches the house was always dark, shadowed by the steep valley behind it. The day I discovered her, it was late autumn. Blue skies and bitter-cold. I'd walked home from school along the soggy canal path, which was dappled with leaves and goose-shit. By this time, Mum had withdrawn from the house entirely, taking to her room. She said it was because of the illness. She needed to rest a lot, she said. But I suppose it also meant she could carry on drinking without us seeing. I only saw her in weird snatches then, in her last few months, in our secret congresses after school. Mum suddenly wanted to tell me all these things about herself. She'd never been much of a storyteller before. But now, I was routinely summoned and she'd pour it all out at break-neck speed, all these stories about the past. I'd come into the house, climb the dark stairs, and knock tentatively at her door, Moira's door. Mum had always insisted I refer to her by her first name. But I called her "Mum" secretly, in my head and whenever she was out of range.

Mum's room was a long oblong space: two bedrooms had been repurposed, when my parents bought the house, to become a small dance studio. The studio had large windows along one side that opened onto the canal and the opposite wall was mirrored. The mirror reflected the canal, spilling its green, dank light through the space; I used to think that my mother was like a fish, trapped inside a tank that was never cleaned. There were shelves of books at the far end of the room and, against the mirror-wall, a rotting chaise longue that Mum reclined on, winding herself in cashmere blankets. Next to the chaise longue was a small, black, lacquered cabinet, which held Mum's curiosities: an assortment of exquisite glassware — frosted lilac martini glasses, curlicue champagne flutes, etched sherry glasses, crystal tumblers, a tiny cube of glass with a battered silver lid — and sticky bottles of strange spirits. There were white rings on the top of the cabinet, where residual vodka had scoured the lacquer off the surface, and this used to make me think of the illness, of Mum's liver, blanched and retracting. There was sometimes a small plate of garnishes that she would offer me enthusiastically, as though she had baked a cake. For her last few months, Mum ate only olives, glacé cherries and curled orange rind, as far as I could tell.

Sometimes she was on wonderful form. She would usher me in and immediately set off on a story, as though she was restarting a conversation from a moment before. She told me her history as though she was recounting it to a journalist, balancing facts with appealing, atmospheric detail. Moira had, for a fleeting period in the late 1970s, been a promising ballerina. This was when she had met Vincent, my father, after her first starring performance. He was, by the end, her oldest, most devoted and only remaining fan. When they had first met, she had been surrounded by interested parties. During her one run as Odette, there had been a buzz around Moira; her performance had been received with excitement and people suddenly wanted to know her, to interview her, to take her picture in the rehearsal room. But Moira's problems had also begun. That shady region of pain, the dull, grey fuzz at the front of her knees, had become much worse. She had danced through it, and during the later performances it had reached a pitch of exquisite intensity, shooting through her kneecaps. She had iced her joints each evening at midnight. And Moira had prided herself on being able to keep going, dancing through it; her dying finale had become more and more convincingly agonised. But after the show had finished, one night she found she could barely walk. The stairs to her flat had become almost impossible. The academy provided several different kinds of "conservative" treatment: they manipulated, palpitated and injected her kneecaps. But these interventions all failed in turn and they decided on surgical correction. Through the long months of incapacity in her pale green bedsit in Islington, my father, Vincent Freestone, made himself indispensable. After that first performance, he had asked if he might visit her; she was delighted to discover that alongside being a journalist he was an expert on classical music, and a real friendship developed. He was an odd young man, she said, there was no denying that: slightly overweight, always dressed in an ill-fitting knitted tank-top and a flat cap, which he held against his heart when he sat at her bedside. There was a gruffness in his manner towards other people which bordered on the rude; but this made his tender attentions to her come to seem more dependable than the easy, effusive sympathy of her dance friends. And he brought her the most surprising and wonderful gifts: black-cherry yoghurts, orchids, instant coffee, chocolates filled with liquor. He made her whiskey sours and always brought new classical records for them to listen to. After the privations of dance school, spending time with him felt like being at a clandestine midnight feast.

When the third operation failed to restore Moira's right knee, my father had proposed. He had been offered a good job at a newspaper back up in Yorkshire; he would be able to take care of her. They could buy a house big enough for a studio and Moira could teach, he said. And she'd be closer to her people, who were mostly in the North East. Moira had thanked him and told him she would think it over. During her year of invalidism, she had received three other proposals. Moira knew herself to be extremely beautiful; she had been told this tartly by the teachers at dance school as a kind of admonishment. But she was just now realising that she had the kind of appeal to men that was heightened by indisposition. And these prior proposals had been delivered in terms that she felt failed to do her justice. "You're really frightfully pretty, you know," one retired dancer had told her, fingering his moustache and proffering a tiny ring. "You were a terrifically gifted dancer; the next big thing that isn't," her choreographer had said, patting her arm sadly, and producing a little burgundy box. Unlike other young dancers who took compliments badly, Moira was not embarrassed by these aggrandisements. She was, in fact, offended by their diminishments. These compliments fell far short of the colossal and chthonic beauty Moira felt her person comprised. After she'd had a few sours, Moira would sometimes stare at herself hard in the mirror, and she saw, in those glassy violet eyes, the dying swan stare back at her, in all its animal magnificence. "Pretty" didn't come close. She had dismissed these suitors out of hand. But she considered Vincent's proposal seriously. She and Vincent had never so much as kissed and he paid her no direct compliments at all; but to his quiet devotion she imputed an adoring acknowledgement of her catastrophic beauty. He might now, she began to think, be the most discerning audience she could hope to captivate. And so she accepted. She moved with Vincent to Todmorden, where she quickly tired of trying to teach leaden Yorkshire girls to dance; she had a baby and retreated into a gorgeous gloom.

Of course, as soon as I was old enough, she tried to

teach me to dance. But, she told me, I had no natural talent. She could try as hard as she liked and I would only ever be mediocre. I had no grace, so there was little point. When she stopped my lessons, the occasional trips we made to the Leeds Grand became even more occasional. And things seemed to decline more rapidly after that. She barely spoke to my father, and when she saw me in the house, she regarded me with distant fondness.

But then our afternoon salons had begun. Sometimes when I arrived home after school, Mum would play records and sweep about the room, blankets still clutched around her, talking through the dances and reminiscing. The afternoon before, the penultimate afternoon, she had put on Prokofiev's *Romeo and Juliet*, turning it all the way up until I could feel the music in my body. Perhaps you know the music? It begins with the rising panic of the flutes. And then the rest of the orchestra builds up towards the enormous crash, which is followed by an eerie softness, the lingering harp, the weird violin screech. The music is like moving water then, pooling towards another vast swell. At this point in the music, Mum dropped her blanket dramatically to the floor. She rose up on her feet and they began to flutter beneath her. "You see," she shouted, "she's falling in love. The bourrée is like the fluttering of Juliet's heart." She fluttered a while longer; and then she clutched at pieces of the furniture and slowly lowered herself backwards. "*This* is being moved," she cried, as she arched her spine, her long white neck bared and the crown of her head descending towards the floor. Her hand swept across her brow. "I swoon," she cried out, her voice constricted. "And it must be spectacular; I stay like this until the dizziness blanks everything out. All I can feel is the arch of my back and the rush towards the floor. I am *almost* gone. And then he will swoop to catch me." Here she dragged herself up, grasping the shelves of the bookcase, until her body was stacked back up to vertical. "I will surrender my weight to him now, and he will take his cargo." She was breathless. She fell back onto her chaise longue and took her amber-green drink. "There is no falling in love without the swoon. The backbend, the sink and then the lift in his arms. *This* is the key to classical ballet. This is what the surge of the music dictates. *La Sylphide*, our oldest romance, ends with a devastating swoon." Mum put down her glass and moved her hands about her in a fluid distraction. "You know The Sylph? My earthly lover binds me in a scarf; I let him wind it all around me, trembling at its touch; and my wings fall to the ground. He has killed me, you see, without knowing what he has done, and I have let him. I keel over into his arms." She dropped her arms suddenly and let her head fall back, lifeless. "And then I am carried away by my fairy sisters." She slowly circled her head back up and fixed her eyes on the green water beyond the room. "He has *killed me*," she said again, turning to me. "Do you understand?"

I nodded, dumbly, not understanding.

Mum turned back towards the still green water. "When Margot Fonteyn played Juliet, the balcony scene, she managed eighteen swoons in six minutes. It got even more desperate in the bedroom: *thirty-two* swoons. Romeo has to clutch her by the waist, to keep her from falling, doomed, to the floor. *Sleeping Beauty. The Dying Swan.* Imagine these without the backbend? She is extravagance itself; she takes up the whole stage with her swooning. With her dying. And then there is *Giselle!*" Her hands swept about in mesmerised movements. "I fall in love with a duke so deeply that it takes all my strength. I am so fragile, I flutter on the breeze. I hear of his marriage to another and I am driven mad. I sink and swoon in my doomed adagios. And I die, but *still* I dance. I rise up from my grave, with the other jilted harpies, who wreak revenge upon their faithless men. But I will have no revenge. I will dance again with my Duke and forgive him; I swoon back into the forest, back to my grave." She sighed and laid her arms above her head, sinking deeper into the chaise. Her eyes were closed. This was the sign that I was dismissed.

The next day, I climbed the stairs and knocked at Mum's door and there was no answer. I knocked again and she uttered an abyssal sound. I sloped away and tried to do my biology homework, but the anxiety built into a flutter that forced me to move about. I was almost dancing. I alternated between the upstairs rooms, listening for any signs of life. There was nothing; not even the sound of glasses and bottles clinking. I loitered outside her room, knocked again. I couldn't shake the gruesome thought of her bleeding out silently into the red velvet. I pushed the door open. My mother's arms hung limply either side of the chaise longue. Her back was pushed up along the curve of the recliner and her pretty head hung backwards, eyes open, hair sweeping the floor. She was utterly still, resolved in a perfect swoon.

III
Falling in Love

I practised, often. Breathing quickly, then holding my breath, over and over again. Long after Leanne and Laura and all the others had forgotten about the game, I was becoming adept at it. I learnt to recognise when to stop if I wanted a headrush; and how to push myself over. I had a square of cashmere blanket, from Mum's old room, which I kept under my pillow. I suppose you might think it maudlin. Some evenings, I would begin with that little fabric square, holding it, feeling its scratchy softness against my cheek. Then I would lie back on my bed and close my eyes, allowing the greenness to begin to fill them up. I would listen to the empty house, ticking around me. I would quicken my breath in successive cycles, and then I would take one enormous breath in and expel it fully. I would seal my mouth shut. My thoughts would begin to thin down and I'd arch my body upwards, like a fish. Sometimes I'd come back up almost immediately, gasping, my body rippling for oxygen as though I'd been beached. But other times I'd go under. I don't know for how long; time gets strange under the water. I'd think of her and I'd let my body swim.

I thought she might like it if I fell in love. That was supposed to be the way it happened, after all, the proper way: like Juliet and Odette and the Sylph and Giselle. And that was how people talked about it, too: falling, falling hard, falling apart. So I hurled myself at romance, wanton with vertigo. The summer I turned fifteen, Aaron Murgatroyd, Laura's brother, started giving me lifts in his car. He hung around the school gates waiting for me, and Leanne and the others wore even more make-up and lurid bras that showed through their thin white shirts in hot pink, neon yellow, leopard print. Aaron was nineteen, a painter-decorator by day and a boxer by night; he spat a lot and had little scars on his hands. His skin was dark, but he had the lightest green eyes. He looked at the other girls in their tiny skirts as though they were the most boring sight imaginable, occasionally delivering them an ostentatious yawn. But whenever he spotted me through the railings he half-smiled, and I spotted it; then he would kick the ground to make the smile go away and walk mock-nonchalant towards the car, slightly ahead of me. He sometimes had a bag of chips waiting for me, making the front seat warm and salty-damp when I sat on it in my school skirt.

Some evenings he would drive us up onto the moor. The further up the valley sides you go, the weirder the place names become: we drove through Little Egypt, past the row of exposed cottages called the Walls of Jericho; we drove along Pudding Lane and wandered round the Red Water in the violet gloaming; we drove up Dog House and stopped at Scald End. And one night we drove up Sour Hall Lane, over cattle grids, along unmade tracks, all the way to Flower Scar, the old Roman road that tracks up to the very top of the Pennines. We were sat right at the peak of the valley, eating our chips wi' bits and drinking pop the colour of anti-freeze. We never said much to one another. The sun had just vanished from sight. In one direction, you could see all the way down the valley to Pendle, the hills beginning to turn blue in the dusk. In the other direction, the valley split in two, forking away towards Hebden Bridge and Rochdale. Studley Pike, blackened and phallic, rose out of the tops.

Aaron swigged on his can. Little lights began to glimmer, like tiny stars caught in the valley sides. "Esther," he said, continuing to look straight ahead. "Ettie, I think about you all the time." He looked ashamed and stared at the steering wheel; then he hit it hard with both his hands. "Look, do you want to or not?"

I looked outwards, to the different distances of dark blue. Then I looked back at Aaron, at his dark profile. "Yeah, all right," I said.

Aaron was almost instantly on top of me and my skirt ruched all the way up. I felt a slight rush and I concentrated on it: I closed my eyes, I thought about Juliet and I tried to hear the music, the weird violin screech and then the pooling swell. I let my head fall backwards, to constrict my throat. But I couldn't get the breathing quite right. I opened my eyes and looked out again, across the valley. Those hills, vanishing to darkness, were once on the same latitude as the Port of Sudan and Santiago de Cuba. You could have walked all the way from the Flower Scar to the South Pole on dry land. Mr Nield, with his long face and his desperate eyes, told us this in Geography class. Way back in *deep* time, hundreds of millions of years ago, the world existed as one enormous landmass, a Pangaea, surrounded by sea. The land had slowly, so slowly, riven apart, drifted imperceptibly into the continents we now know. Of all the cycles of the earth, the seasons, the tides, day and night, this was the most dramatic: the earth was breaking up, pulling apart. And in the future, in hundreds more millions of years, it would collide again, recombining in a new supercontinent, and the shape of this new world would be totally unrecognisable. When I let myself go entirely, when I played dead in the dark, I could sometimes feel the earth move, a slow violent tremor through the ground below me. And this made me feel even more dizzy. There had been time, Mr Nield said, since the beginning of the universe, for it all to have come and gone, and come and gone again. The only traces of these vanished worlds would be the atoms inside us, atoms formed in stellar explosions. And this universe too would end: the sun would die and geological time would run out. I closed my eyes again and let the dizzying deepen. I hyperventilated, quietly, so that Aaron wouldn't notice. I was just beginning to swoon away, when suddenly Aaron collapsed on top of me. He *ugged*, and then he reared up, before dropping himself back heavily into the driver's seat. He fixed his clothes, he cleared his throat, and then he opened the window onto the cool night sky and he spat out into it. And there we were again. Two damply separate human globs; bits of stars with blinking eyes.

IV
Communal Narcotics

I kept trying to find romance with Aaron. But he always seemed to interrupt me. Sometimes I'd swoon too soon, before he got properly started, and he'd get angry and tell me to stop playing silly beggars. On my sixteenth birthday, Aaron took me for a drive and proposed. I laughed uncontrollably. He snatched the ring-box back into his pocket and looked at me for a moment in bleak confusion, before telling me to get out of the car. I spent that evening walking home along the side of the bypass. And after that, Aaron stopped driving me up onto the tops: he said I must have some kind of altitude sickness, with all the dizziness. We occasionally went for curry and beer in the valley bottom, but I could tell he half hated me now. Most nights I was alone in the house. Dad worked even later hours and I would often lie on her bed, holding my breath in the dark, listening to the house creak, drifting in and out. Sometimes I felt her, as I arched my body upwards, as a slight shiver. Then I'd swoon fully.

I did well in my A-levels. I think the de-oxygenation made me especially receptive to Romantic poetry and I took up a place at the University of Leeds to study Literature. I made the journey across to the city several times a week, taking the train that cuts through the bottom of the valley and speeds its landscape past. There was a boy on my course, Rufus, who smelled of hemp and mouldering grass. He sat next to me in poetics seminars, and he always lolloped alongside me afterwards, trying to get me to delay the journey back to Todmorden and come to the pub. We often sat together in the Dry Dock, a beached barge-turned-bar in the middle of the ring road, drinking bitter and making jokes. Despite his ambient odour and crumpled appearance, Rufus betrayed his background almost immediately: he had been educated at Harrow and his parents were academics. They had made a large amount of money designing psychometric tests for the recruitment purposes of big companies. Rufus would tell me about his agonising holidays back home from school, when his every word was silently noted by his parents. He was convinced they were chalking everything up for later analysis. He told me that he became almost silent, for a while. And even at university, he often blushed deeply when he spoke, his sonorous voice seeming to act against his will.

In our final year, Rufus invited me to move into a squatted house in Chapel Allerton. Dad didn't want me to go. But it would just be for a year and I barely saw my father at home anyway. I persuaded him that I needed to be out in the world; the truth was, I was beginning to feel ready for an audience. The Cherry Street house was well-organised. There were grilles on the front windows, so that the light came in in dingy perforations, but otherwise it was perfectly homely. The couple who had cracked the house open lived in the ground-floor living-room. They were Bradford anarchists who survived on food recovered from supermarket skips. Each evening they would go out into Leeds, kitted out like renegade poachers: khaki jackets, combats, netted bags, adrenaline-readied to leap walls and dangle over the edge of the massive food bins, fishing for deformed bagels and use-by expired mackerel. They would bring back their catch and improvise exquisite meals: trout with poached eggs and roasted beetroot; pork with bruised peaches and goat's cheese; serrano ham and celeriac hash; all washed down with a chablis lifted from the Tesco Metro. In what might once have been the dining room lived a Danish journalist, Begitte, who wrote about the evils of the capitalist property market and the ethical necessity of squatting. She spoke several languages fluently and lived almost entirely on raw food. Upstairs was Rufus' room, which was filled with books and photographs and records, and the occasional beautiful girl draped over his furniture in her underwear, hazed in smoke. Next to him was a box-room where Jay, a near-silent heroin addict, slept in a methadone swoon. And across the hall from them was my room.

When I arrived, a brutal-looking dog stood guarding the door: a pit-bull cross, black with a white patch across one eye and shoulders wider than mine. Rufus ruffled the dog's ears, in a not-altogether-convincing way. "It's Jay's dog. The house dog now, I suppose. Jay doesn't really get out to walk him, so we take him out when we can. Good boy, Braxus."

The dog pushed its enormous head against my thigh and whined effetely. I nudged past it.

My room was at the back of the house, so there were no grilles on the windows. The roof sloped down to a mattress against the back wall. The walls were painted orange and the room smelled of warm bodies and wood. I loved it. For almost a year, I slept and read and drank and passed out in that room, looking out on the cherry trees on the back street and listening to Peter Green's Fleetwood Mac on repeat. Aaron came to visit occasionally and always looked bewildered. He brought round buckets of fried chicken and pleaded with me to come back to the Calder Valley.

On weekends, I used to go dancing with Rufus and I made a point of ingesting everything that I was offered. I was learning about the world beyond the valley, and this seemed like good manners. We used to go to the West Indian Centre and listen to dub played so loudly that I could feel my internal organs throb at their different resonating frequencies. Sometimes this would be too much of a temptation. I'd begin to let go in the bobbing frenzy of dreadlocks and sweat and adrenaline. I'd close my eyes and begin to look for the green light behind them. I'd feel my vibrating pancreas, making me nauseously conscious of the separate parts of my body, of my private densities. And then I'd begin to go — I'd feel the swoop in my stomach and everything would go wonderfully blurry. But Rufus got sick of the bouncers forcing him to take me outside. He said I needed to learn my limits, and he invited me out less and less often.

During the week, I would read and read, and Braxus would loll with his massive head on my lap, drooling on my knees as I worked my way through two centuries of haunted novels. The pace at which I read was ferocious, but I retained next to nothing. It began to feel like the words were so much dark water running through my brain; nothing of it remained, but it flowed on through, and the process of losing it felt as though it might be keeping me alive. The more I read, the worse I did in my essays.

I'd brought the square of cashmere blanket from my mother's old room with me and I kept it under my pillow. My talent was well developed by now. In my room, I would begin by caressing the cashmere, feeling its scratchy softness against my skin. I had a sort of ritual, I suppose. I would lean back and close my eyes, allowing the greenness to begin to fill the dark. The light from outside would gleam against my closed eyelids, like a pulsing phosphorescence. I always tried to hear the music; sometimes I even played the music: the screech of the violins, the pooling, overwhelming swell. And I would arch my spine, letting me head fall all the way back, to constrict my throat more quickly. Sometimes I would hang off the edge of the bed, dangling my head upside down. On a good day, everything would soften instantly at the edges, and I'd be able to see her clearly in my mind's eye and feel my body doubling hers. On a bad day, I'd pass out too quickly to feel her and I'd come to with Braxus licking my cheeks.

In the spring, the squat started to prickle up in agitation. There were rallies in town against the privatisation of higher education and Rufus and the anarchists joined an occupation of the University's buildings. I felt a strange sort of tingling excitement about all of this; that it might be another chance to act on a larger stage, as part of some sort of ensemble. I tagged along with Rufus to various meetings and marched alongside him in a demonstration. I let my body get crushed into the body of people. There was a thrill to this — the way a woman's shoulder pushed right up against mine, again and again, and the woman didn't even notice, or if she did, she let it carry on, shoulder to shoulder — that made me feel a little dizzy. I spent a couple of broken nights sleeping on the floor of a conference centre, where I breathed in the carpet dust and listened to people chatting on the balcony and playing guitar through the night. Rufus knew everyone in the movement; in fact he'd slept with most of the girls. He often spoke at length in the group discussions, while everyone sat round in a circle using occult hand-signals. Rufus' face bloomed whenever he orated; he looked truly happy. Other people seemed to instantly trust him by his blush and he became a sort of de facto leader. Messages of support started to pour in: writers, academics and broadcasters sent their solidarity and came to give talks in the evenings. People baked us cakes and braved the University's intimidating security staff to deliver them. It turned out that Rufus was incredibly well-connected: journalists, professors, past MPs, all came to address us at his invitation. The real coup was Rufus' godfather: the famous poet and 'personality' H.E. Ruthen announced that he would launch his new collection, with all attendant publicity, from the sit-in. He arrived one evening with a terrified publisher and wandered round the space, talking to the great unwashed with evident pleasure. He was an enormous man: six feet six and broad across the shoulders, but narrowed to nothing in his waist and the pits of his cheeks. He wore a velvet jacket and a cravat, and had a booming, patrician voice.

The room had filled up in expectation of his reading, until hundreds were crushed into the space. Rufus gave out specific directions in the case of a fire, because the University had blockaded our fire escapes. Someone from the crowd shouted, "Corporate murder," and everyone cheered. Ruthen began with a long address on the importance of dialectics to poetry. He talked about the contradictions that are endemic to society and to language. He talked about the need to access these conflicts, to give them full scope, in poetry and in political action, so that language and society might transform themselves. He told us that acts of resistance were works of art. He told us that the fight began here, that we must carry it on to save education and the hope of a more egalitarian society. We must resist the changes that had been made since the Browne Review and the invasion of the neo-liberal body snatchers. And then he read his new poems to rapturous applause.

Afterwards, Ruthen's publisher hovered at a desk with his books set out, and Ruthen held court, signing copies and clapping some occupiers on the back. Rufus produced a bottle of cava he'd smuggled in and we toasted the new collection with plastic cups. I skittered about at the edges of the group. There was something unsettling about the way Ruthen kept looking at me, as he boomed to the group. When people asked him questions, about his poetry, or his politics, he had a way of shutting them down with a joke, of dismissing them, or of humouring them but letting everyone else see how utterly facile he thought they were. This didn't seem very dialectical. The evening wore on: he sat down and students circled about him. He kept swivelling around, staring at each person as they spoke, seeming to hold them in a kind of indulgent contempt. His nostrils flared. He snorted unabashedly at some comments, as he signed his books. And his eyes kept lighting on me. He looked down his nose, as though sighting me down the barrel of a gun. Rufus laughed horribly at everything he said. The publisher had sold all the books and was beginning to ready Ruthen for departure. Everyone wanted to shake his hand before he left. As he made his way past me, he swooped suddenly and grabbed me hard by the upper arm: "Hawk seeks mouse," he said, right into my inner ear. "Meet me outside in ten minutes." He dropped my arm just as suddenly and shook more hands on his way out.

After that, I curled up in a corner. I watched the main occupation leaders at the front of the room making plans for the next day, deciding who to invite for the Friday night slot. Two of them knew famous comedians and the group was now arguing about which of the two was the more radical and who would draw the larger crowd. I wanted to leave. The excitement of the first march was gone. It was all individuals now: the power of their personal charisma to persuade. I could sneak out to quiver in the dark, clutching at tree bark, letting Ruthen turn me to quarry. But it all seemed like a rather tired scenario. I would be acting out a hammy part. And what kind of audience wants to see that? Not a very discerning one. I spent a few more hours there in the occupation; and then, when it was safe, I ventured back out into the city.

The next few months I stayed away from the action: I heard reports from Rufus, when he occasionally came back home for the night. I spent a lot of time in my room. I read and I wrote in the day, and I drank and I passed out in the evenings. The nights were getting warmer, the sky was brightening. One evening in May, I walked back along Cherry Street with a stack of books, breathing in the smell of lit pollen and beer rising from the students smoking and drinking in their front gardens. But when I arrived at the front door, a policewoman was barring the way.

"Do you live here?" the woman asked. Her voice was kind, despite her military stance.

"I do," I said.

"Then we're going to need to ask you a few questions."

Another officer ushered me through to the kitchen and asked me to sit down. The other doors were shut, but I could hear unfamiliar steps in the room above — in my room. And the house smelled strange: of metal and salt.

The officer explained, firmly and in deliberately simple terms, the basic outline of what had happened, with timings and locations cross-referenced against his notebook. I elaborated the scene in my mind as the officer stirred sugar into a cup of tea that would apparently help me with the shock. Begitte had raised the alarm at 15:07. She had been working at her desk that afternoon, researching an article. Seemingly out of nowhere, a small orb of bright liquid had dropped onto her page. It had spread slowly into a bright orange circle on the paper, working its way through the grain. And then another drop had followed. And another. Begitte had looked up. A livid patch of reddish brown was bleeding across the ceiling above her, a bright, asymmetric bulge of colour either side of a line in the plasterboard. It was darkest at the centre, spreading to bright orange at the edges, as though the plasterboard were litmus. She had no idea what it could be. A break in a pipe that was full of liquid rust? A psychedelic attack of liquid legionnaires? And there was a smell to it. A smell of iron and salt.

Exsanguinated. That was the word, the word I repeated in my mind over and over. I wanted to give the officer the word. Perhaps he didn't know it? It swelled in my mouth, unspoken. Exsanguinated. The fatal loss of all the blood from the body. Jay had slit his wrists. And he'd done it properly, scoring vertically along from the tender crux behind the elbow all the way to the wrist. He had slumped against the wall and bled his way out into the floorboards, along the joists, through the plasterboard, and down onto Begitte's white page. He had sat there, emptying, until Begitte discovered him.

"I'm afraid we recovered some drugs paraphernalia in your friend's room. So we need to conduct a search of the rest of the property."

"Where's Braxus?" I asked.

"Braxus?" the policeman echoed.

"The dog. Jay's dog."

The policeman looked at the table.

"We did discover a dog at the property. But I'm afraid it had to be confiscated under the Dangerous Dogs Act."

"Confiscated?"

"Miss, the dog is illegal. It will need to be destroyed."

When they'd finished their search, I retrieved the cashmere square from the back of my bedroom door, and left everything else behind. I walked down the pollen-hazed street towards town. I took the train to Todmorden and walked back along the canal path. It was a soft, warm evening. I knocked at the front door. My father had Wagner on in the living room and had unbuttoned his shirt, so that his stomach domed out.

"Esther," he said, staring at me. "Whatever have you done to yourself?" He opened the door and then stood watching as I walked back up the stairs to her room. "I knew you'd come back," he called out after me.

V
Big City

A year later, I was stagnating at the bottom of the valley. I'd been doing some temp work at my Dad's paper and I was feeling listless. I could turn myself out like a light, now, but there was no one to see it, no one to know how beautifully my act had developed. I knew where she had gone for her audience. I wanted to do the same.

Dad drove me down at the start of the summer. We navigated our way on the M1 and then turned into the intestinal streets of the city. In the last stages of the journey, the car moved slowly along a road in south London and a heat-haze streamed upwards from the stationary traffic ahead of us, making a zigzag of fumes on the air. I'd been to London once as a child, she brought me here one Christmas, to see *The Nutcracker*. This looked nothing like my memories of Covent Garden. I stared out of the open car-window, watching the procession of people and things as they trailed past. White boys with mean, thin bodies were strutting, shirtless, on the garage forecourt to the right. One of them yanked a squat dog on a lead that had been improvised from string. A gang of children jostled for position outside the newsagent, smoking and swearing competitively. Tables lined the pavement in front of shops, offering up boxes full of mangoes and arthritic-looking vegetables. In the windows, naked halal chickens hung by the score.

"What do you think of it, then?" Dad asked as we crept down the high street. I didn't say anything. But I was excited. From the paranoid look of the men gathered outside the mobile phone shop, to the unfeasibly pink pool of freshly-ejected sick at the end of my new street, to the violent movement of people and vehicles in every direction; it all comprised a completely new scene.

"Dad," I cried, "turn here. This is it." We turned onto Denmark Terrace, passed the white facades of the Victorian terraces, and pulled up at number 29. I had very little with me. On the back seat of my father's car sat a carrier bag with some shoes in it, two carrier bags full of clothes, and another carrier bag of toiletries. I gathered these things together and then stood next to my father on the doorstep. He rang the bell. There was a small front garden, with two overgrown rose bushes coming into bloom. An old climber, desiccated now, was still twisted over the door and up the front of the house. We heard heavy footfall on the stairs inside and then my cousin appeared at the door.

"Hello. Esther. Uncle Vince." Veronica raised her right hand. She didn't smile exactly, but stretched her mouth outwards horizontally. She stood for a moment on the threshold, eyeing me up, as though she might have thought better of the whole thing. But then she ushered us inside, towards the dark kitchen at the back of the house. Dad leant against a worktop, testing surfaces with a tap of his nails, like an undercover surveyor. I stood close to him, still clutching my carrier bags. I wasn't sure if I should make myself at home just yet. Veronica put the kettle on and asked us about our journey. Veronica was a junior doctor. She is a solid person, certain of her usefulness to the world, socially at ease. I recalled a childhood family trip to a stately home: I had sloped off with Veronica, thinking we were drawn together into a cousinly conspiracy, and then she had forced me to climb a tree, standing below me with a long, sharp stick and pricking my thighs whenever I stopped moving. This, Veronica had said, was to toughen me up.

"Listen, Esther, make yourself at home. I've got to dash to a shift, but I've had these keys cut for you, and your room's right at the top. Sorry I can't stay, old man." Veronica batted Dad on the arm. "Duty calls." And then she was out through the front door.

I liked my new room. It reminded me of the squat, because of the slope of the roof and the smell of wood. It only took me a few moments to unpack. I came back downstairs to find my father poking about in the kitchen. There were stacks of filthy crockery around the sink and half-eaten things had been abandoned on the worktops. There was a distinct smell of mouse. "If this is how doctors live," Dad said, "I wouldn't want them anywhere near my viscerals, eh?" He emitted a short laugh. "Let's go out for dinner, love."

We set off on foot back towards the main road, wading through the warm evening and the smell of petrol. At the end of the road, a man was sitting on the ground against the wall of a Cambodian takeaway and fish-and-chip shop, sweating, in a filthy jacket. He had ejected a new puddle of vomit. Dad upped the pace towards Tooting.

We opted for a Sri Lankan restaurant with bamboo place

mats. We ordered too much food; Dad was being beneficent. He told to me to dig in, but I could see he was slightly horrified when I kept on going. I downed four large bottles of beer and then I ordered us spirits. He was studying my face: my lurid orange lipstick, which had probably smudged and sometimes left a bright wax on my teeth; my hair, a dull mink colour, hung heavily around my face; my white cheeks and my almost invisible eyelashes. Sometimes, when I don't wear mascara, my eyes look sort of derelict. I could see Dad was finding it painful to appraise my face. He'd like me to be well-groomed, like her.

"Will you think about the job, love?" Dad had got me the chance of a journalism internship with a local paper back in Yorkshire, and I had refused it. Instead I'd accepted a temp receptionist job at the *Ham and High* in north London, a newspaper with no connection to my father. "You don't have to do something so menial."

"I want to try this," I said. I downed my final drink and then we headed back towards Veronica's house. We stopped at a crossing on the main road and Dad pressed the button. Cars and motorbikes sped past at a furious pace, relentless even on a Sunday evening.

"Just a minute," I said. I felt a little peculiar. I thought I might be about to spontaneously pass out; that had never happened before. Perhaps it would be a sign of some kind, from her? But instead, as the green man started to beep, I threw up my entire meal into the road.

"Oh, Esther, love." Dad bent down to help me. "Esther. I don't want to leave you here."

But I reared back up, laughing wildly. Everything was so new and I couldn't wait to perform here. "There's nowhere else I'd rather be." I spat into the gutter and then linked his arm, zig-zagging him all the way back to the house.

It took ages to get rid of him. We searched out coffee in the gloomy, mousy cupboards, and once this was finished, nothing could legitimately delay him. He stood on the doorstep of 29 Denmark Terrace, and he caught me by the wrist.

"Let me see your eyes, love." He tilted my face up towards him. He was doing this to try to see her, I knew, because our eyes share the same strange colour; a milky grey that she called violet.

He let go of my chin. "Esther, London's a big place. It's different. If anyone ever hurts you Esther, you tell me. You tell me and…" He sniffed hard and pushed his thumb and forefinger against his eyelids.

I stared up at the sky. His performance was making me think of the night of my mother's funeral when, after everyone else had gone, I was left in the front room with Dad, fully alone with him for the first time. A new compact of two. He had been drinking enough to make him weepy. He had taken my hand. "Esther," he had said, staring into the fireplace. "Esther, I sometimes have the strangest thoughts. Sometimes I want someone to hurt you, Esther. Only a little. So that I can hurt them back. So that I can protect you. I tried to protect her, I really did..." And then he had dropped my hand, leant back into the sofa and pressed his thumbs into his eyes, sniffing violently.

He had stopped sniffing now, on the doorstep of 29 Denmark Terrace, after a few long moments. "You've got a big journey, Dad," I said.

"Yes, of course. I'll go." He kissed me, holding me tight to him, and then he moved away down the path. At the gate he turned back towards me. His body was black against the navy sky.

"I have been a good father, haven't I, Esther?" he called out.

"Yes, Dad," I said and slammed the door shut.

I ran straight up to my new room, in the eaves, and opened the skylights, letting in the warm night air. I lay on the bed, listening for the sound of my father's car pulling away. I thought of her and slowed my breathing, only half swooning. When I was very young, on Sunday nights we sometimes drove along the motorway in the darkness, coming back from my Nana's house. I would look out into the blackness and see the glimmering squares of light from houses in nearby towns. I would always want Dad to turn off the road, to pull up so that I could get out, knock on each door and introduce myself. It was such a strange thought, that there were all these people, inside their houses, eating their teas and making jokes and sitting on their sofas, who knew nothing about us, who didn't know about my beautiful mother, and would never know that we had been there, secretly in the dark, speeding past them, seeing their windows and wondering about them.

And now, lying in my new bed, I thought of all the people in London, living in parallel, their rooftops multiplying away towards the city centre. I was thinking that most would never know, or even wonder about me. I could chalk them up as parallel lines on a wall and they would repeat away, exceeding my ability to mark them, because of all the new people being born. And even though I couldn't count them, we were all in the city together, at the same time, duplicating one another. I was joining them, just like she had before me; we were all lying in parallel. I sank further into the bed and began to make myself dizzier. When I slept, I dreamed of falling.

VI

Empathic Ocean

The next morning, I sat on the black line for the very first time. In the beginning, the Tube felt to me like one of those rickety fairground rides that you don't quite trust: noisily pulling away from each station, juddering with effort at first, then gaining speed, hurtling onwards to the next stop. Newspapers, umbrellas, rucksacks, jackets, coffee cups and portable pots of porridge pushed against me at every turn. I felt fantastically violated. I marvelled at each station as the fit-to-burst carriage squeezed in an extra couple of people. It reminded me of my father's old party trick — he would slip five-pence pieces into an already brimming pint, squeezing the metal discs down the inside of the glass, the ale rising to a dome in the middle as more and more pieces were artfully eased in, seeming to defy the laws of space. I closely watched the new people around me: sitting opposite was an older woman in festival-bright lycras, staring ahead and out of the window at the furred black insides of the Tube tunnel, a beatific look on her face; a smartly-dressed young woman sat diagonally opposite, skinny, jittery, her movements like a hunted bird's; and next to her sat a jaundiced-looking man, sweat puckering on his upper lip, a slight agitation to his face, staring intently at the young woman's ballet pumps next to his own feet. I changed onto the grey line at London Bridge, alongside lots of the same passengers. We moved together through the station tunnels like a school of fish, finally taking our places in a new carriage. A couple of moments in and a strong smell prickled my nostrils. I thought at first that a dog must have squeezed its way onto the train, between the legs of the densely-packed passengers. I glanced to my right: a large man in a high-vis jacket was pushing his way through to catch hold of a pole. His hair was lank and his chin was stubbled: dense iron filings worked into circles by magnets. He stood right in front of me and I could practically see the smell coming off him in mustardy waves. I turned to watch the other passengers: a woman standing nearby pushed her mouth into a converse arch and turned her head away; another squirmed and put a handkerchief across her face. No one could move away. I settled into my seat and began to breathe deeply. I let my head fall backwards and began the ritual. I closed my eyes and concentrated on the smell. The odour was waxy at first, like lanolin and ears and dirty scalps; and then it stung into something more vinegar and sharply testicular. I breathed in again: finally the smell tanged into mouldering yeast. The man's body was impressing itself on everyone in the carriage. It was obscene. The more I breathed, the stronger the smell became, as though he were blooming in my nose. It was heavy, his scent, and it started to get to me. I breathed in again: dog and cider-groin and thickened scalp-fat, it hit me hard in the sinuses. I thought about my first London swoon being here, on the Tube. But then I started to gag and Swiss Cottage was announced. I got up, followed the jaundiced-looking man up the escalator, fixing my attention on his back, and the way his white shirt clung to the damp column of his spine, all the way to the street.

I pushed through the revolving doors of the newspaper office and into the foyer. The building was glass fronted and the sunshine made the grain of the white marble floor sparkle. It was much grander than anywhere I had temped before. Other people surged in around me, breasting up out of the Tube and on through the building. I approached the front desk. "Hello," I said, "I'm Esther Freestone. I'm the new temp."

"Oh. Right," said the woman on the other side of the desk. She was slightly behind and to the right of a massive flower arrangement that had a pineapple as its centre-piece. The woman half-sighed; it was just audible. "Well, this is your seat." She motioned towards the empty chair behind the counter and I made my way round to it. On my side of the desk there was a computer, a piece of paper with log-in details, an empty desk-tidy, a company mug full of biros and a small stand-alone sign with my name on it, cut into white plastic: Esther Freestone. There was something plasticky bright and biting about my name laid out like that. I sat on the chair and plummeted down a few inches.

"Your chair is slightly temperamental," the woman said. "But *Polly* never had any complaints." She looked straight ahead at her screen and jabbed at her keyboard, her fingernails clack-clacking against the keys. I got the impression that she might not have been typing into a real document; the clacking was quick and defensive. On her side of the desk there was another company mug, this one with a red-brown lipstick pucker on the rim; a photograph of an older man, stood amongst racing dogs; two paperweights, identical except for the colour of the swirls inside; an open packet of Silk Cuts; a small mound of multi-coloured paperclips; and a name plate: Maureen Cooper. She must have been in her late forties: aggressively cropped bleached blonde hair, red nails, mouth drawn on in a fierce red-brown, tight trousers with a satin shirt tucked in, glittering gold and diamante earrings.

"You've got a safety video to watch for the next hour. If you don't get a move on you'll be late for it." She didn't look up from her screen.

The room had no windows. There was shelving on each wall and each shelf was full of packets of paper and envelopes and pens in every colour. It was, in truth, a large stationery cupboard in which someone had set up a TV. A woman from HR had introduced herself earlier and provided a plastic seat for me. She had turned off the lights and made a tired joke about popcorn. Then I sat in the dark and watched a man on the screen lifting things off a pallet: in the right way (knees bent: big green tick); and in the wrong way (bending from the hips: enormous red cross). For a moment I wondered what I was doing here. But then I sank into the dark and let my head fall backwards. I didn't go completely. Just enough to remind me that here, in this enormous city, there would be new ways to let go.

The brightness of the foyer was startling after my sojourn in the cupboard; Maureen Cooper barely acknowledged my return. We sat mostly in silence for the rest of the day, Maureen periodically passing across thick, printed guides to telephony and online systems for me to read. At six o'clock Maureen turned suddenly on me, with a look of some violence. "Right," she said, "we're taking you to the pub." I shut down my computer and followed her out of the building. Maureen lit up almost immediately and we stood on the edge of the busy main road as cars surged past us. Maureen rocked slightly on her heels: from the pleasure of the cigarette, I wondered, or towards the vertiginous pull of the traffic? We were going to "The Swiss", Maureen informed me, between compulsive drags. Maureen's mouth squeezed repeatedly into a bright-brown anus around the end of her fag. I looked away.

The Swiss Cottage pub was directly opposite the office, marooned in an island in the middle of the two streams of traffic where Avenue Road splits. There were four lanes either side and the noise roared around us. We crossed to the pub and Maureen took a seat at a picnic table; its legs were concreted into the solid grey area that was signposted, 'Beer Garden'. "I'll have a white wine soda," Maureen said and pointed me towards the door. Stepping inside the pub was like stepping into another season; it was dark, the tiny windows letting in very little light, like a Black Forest cottage permanently fast in the deep of winter. Several old men sat at the bar, red-nosed, and one nodded at me, swilling his glass. There was an old woman, hunched like a boulder next to an empty fireplace, guarding a tartan wheel-along shopping trolley and a tiny dog. She issued a constant, soft stream of profanities. A Korean man with a sports bag full of knock-off DVDs was winding his way from table to table. Two women stood like henges behind the bar, both of them skinny with blanched faces and gothic lipstick, reluctantly moving to pull pints when called.

I bought the drinks and went back out to the blue sky and car fumes. I sat down next to Maureen and we sank into an uncompanionable silence. Maureen gulped back her drink and chain smoked. "It's warm, no," she said after a while. Some men from the office sat down on a table behind us and Maureen leaned back, pushing into their conversation, asking how they all were, roaring with laughter at their jokes. "I'll have a white-wine soda," she said to one of the men, as he got up. I made my way, alone, back to the bar.

At some point later in the evening, when all the picnic tables were full and the separate parties had spilled over into one another, a man sat down next to me.

"You look a bit lost," he said. He had sandy hair and a sandy face: tan, rough, a gold-blonde greying beard. He was older than me, perhaps in his forties, and his voice lilted upwards, towards the North East.

"Oh, I'm just new here," I said.

"Right," he said. "Do you work at the paper?"

"Sort of," I said. And then, to be whimsical, I offered: "It's a bit like being on a boat here, isn't it?"

"How do you mean?"

"See, we're on the deck of the ship. At the prow." I gesticulated with my glass, describing the shape of the enclosed beer garden, concrete slabs curved into the front of a bow. "And the road rushing around us is the sea."

He looked at me carefully, I could see him assessing the situation, deciding how drunk I was. He didn't seem deterred. "Well, yes," he said, "I can see what you mean. If, of course, you mean the *North* Sea: brimming with pollution and discarded prophylactics and the ghosts of lost souls."

My obligatory laugh seemed to vaporise quickly in the warm night. The sky had sunk into navy blue above and around us and the black tower blocks across the road looked like charred remains on a faraway shore.

"Can I buy you a drink?" he asked.

When he got back, he started telling me about real boats, and his childhood on a quayside. He told me about the area he grew up in and then about its demise. There was something about the emptiness he was describing that I thought I recognised. I wanted to talk more. I thought we might have a rapport; in truth, I thought he might be a good first-night audience.

"We've missed the last Tube," he said. "I know a place we can go."

We lay in bed in a serviced apartment; Thomas had begged the key from a friend who was working the desk of the town-house hotel. We made a post-coital V in the enormous raft of a bed, our feet touching and our bodies angled away from one another. I spent the early morning, as the light broke over London and spilled in through the blinds, making Thomas recount the desolate details of his childhood. I drew the stories out of him. And as he spoke, I closed my eyes, steadily quickening my breath, letting my mind soften.

Thomas told me that he grew up on the Wear at the edge of a Sunderland shipyard, in a terrace of houses at the very limit of the land. When they were still building ships, great steamers would grow up right in front of his front door: 30 feet behind their television set and net curtains, the newest ship would rise straight up, a sheer and incalculable cliff of steel, gradually blocking out the light. The house would be dark for months, he said. And then, on the day of the launch, the freighter's horn would blast and it would be off: sunshine would flood their house again and then the ship-building would start all over. Every so often, at night, Thomas and his sister would wake to the siren's scream: they would peer through the curtains, two tiny faces, to watch the searchlight's beam circle across the surface of the dark water, searching for a lost man.

Thomas's father had been black trade and mostly worked as a welder. He was an incomer, down from Scotland, and he hated it on the yard. And that was before they knew it all, too: how the muck they brought home wasn't just so much oil worked indelibly into carpets and creases of skin, but trails of deadly aerialised poison. Thomas told me how he now imagined it: the asbestos arcing through their house in black stars, mucky sparks cascading through the air from the tips of his father's fingers. Silicosis and asbestosis spread all around the quay. And he wondered now if the black stars were settled at the bottom of his lungs, waiting and growing.

I asked him to tell me about the worst times. I was in a strange breathless state, but one I knew well, holding myself suspended between dizziness and passing out. I could manipulate my breathing so adeptly, by now, that I didn't think he had even noticed.

When things at the yard started to get difficult, he said, his parents started to argue. His father's work was casualised, dwindling to nothing. His mother had grown up in the yards: her father had worked them through the war years, when Sunderland made a quarter of the tonnage of all the ships. Sunderland had won the Second World War, Thomas's grandfather always said. And he'd vowed he'd build ships until he died: which he did, at 55 years-old, when a piece of ironstone fell out of a bucket swinging above his head and shattered his skull.

Their yard was the last to shut finally in 1988. Nothing worse than those ships, Thomas said, except for them being gone. Their house was light now, all the time; but the light was preternaturally bright, carrying seagull cries through the silence into the living room. The quay was deserted and at night, instead of the scream of the siren, he and his sister would wake to the sound of lone, drunken men raging at the water.

After the closure, his mother, Mary, stayed in her room a lot; and then his father, Mick, left them and moved to the South, for new work and a new family. Mick would come back up every so often and sit in his car outside the house, waiting to take Thomas's sister out for her visit. But he never came back inside their poison-star-spangled house. Mick would take

Amanda out for the day and she would come back home with ridiculous presents. They had no money for school dinners or shoes, but Amanda had new earrings and silver bracelets and a ring with a pink, cut-glass stone. Sometimes his mother said Mick didn't take Thomas out with them because Mick was a bastard; but sometimes she said Mick didn't take Thomas out because *Thomas* was a bastard. After a while Thomas stopped hoping for his own visit. His mother didn't do much around the house now; she lived on meal replacement drinks, switching to gin in the evenings, and bought biscuits and cereal for Thomas and his sister. Amanda was desperate to get away. So he tried to keep the house together as best as he could. He learned to cook. By the time he was twelve he could do a mean Vindaloo, with lemon meringue pie for afters. He would persuade his sister to invite her friends over for tea, so that there were more of them and the house would feel full, the noise of them warding off the empty, shipless space outside and the strange glinting light inside. He made lasagne and shepherd's pie and corned beef hash, all out of his paper-round money. His mother sneered and said he had no real skills, not like his grandfather or his father. But his sister and her mates crowded round most evenings, calling him a proper little chef, sometimes kissing him full on the lips and then laughing in his face.

Still, though, his sister wanted to leave. And as soon as she was 16, Amanda left for London. She danced in clubs, she said in a postcard with Beefeaters on the front, and was drinking a lot of champagne. She lived in a flat in Hampstead owned by a very rich man who was in love with her. Their mother tore the postcard into four uneven squares and put them in the bin. His mother drank pink and yellow meal-replacements all day long now, and had grown obese without ever eating solids. Thomas decided that as soon as he was able, he would follow Amanda. He saved his odd-job money and, at 15, took the coach down to London Victoria. But when he got to Mandy's flat it was not what he had expected: there were four girls sharing a bedroom, sleeping on two stained double mattresses on the floor, and when the man who owned the flat came round, she made him hide in a wardrobe. He hated it there and his sister looked tired and sallow; but she swore blind she wouldn't go back North. Thomas spent a couple of weeks sleeping rough on benches on Hampstead Heath, showering back at his sister's, sneaking into the shared bathroom down her corridor. He got a job at a creperie and spent the next 20 years working his way through various kitchens in north London. He managed a coffee shop now, he told me; bought-in cheesecake and frappuccinos. And as he aerated hot milk, he sometimes wondered where the time had gone and how big the dark sparks in his lungs had grown.

Thomas turned over to face me when he'd finished talking. I could feel his eyes on me. I arched up my body and cut off my breath. I started to slide into unconsciousness. "What are you doing, you mad bitch?" he said and he shook me. "Misery porn and a bit of auto-asphyxiation. Is this what you get off on?"

Our rapport wasn't quite what I'd hoped for; but we'd made a start.

That morning was muggy; the warm air nestled round me as I trailed down the Finchley Road towards the office. I was giddy and slightly delirious from lack of sleep. When I sat down behind the reception desk, it was 10:03. Maureen looked over at me and made a clicking sound with her tongue. As everyone streamed into work, I let the Wearside stories continue to circle in my mind, over and over, as I put through calls and booked rooms for meetings. They were beginning to fade already, the details of Thomas's descriptions swirling and changing, becoming secondary to the immediate glass and marble and plastic around me. But something remained strongly in my mind. It was the indulgent weariness in the eyes of the man at the hotel desk last night, as he handed Thomas the keys to the apartment. A suppressed shake of the head and a smothered smile that suggested Thomas's incorrigibility. This cluster of gestures made me think that our evening must have been one of many. That this request for a room had been repeated at least enough times to produce weariness in Thomas's friend.

That my body in that bed, alongside Thomas's, was part of a series of repetitions. From behind the reception desk, I could see the sky above north London turn dark as a bruise. The air was growing humid, fizzing as each besuited visitor drove it in through the revolving doors. It smelled warm and animal, like cat fur. I thought of the city circling close around me, and around Thomas, and around the other bodies that had preceded and would replace me, and him. And I thought of her, as the storm broke in forks of light through the violet sky.

VII

Overpowering Algorithms

A month into the job and nothing spectacular had happened. I had had high hopes of the Tube, at first. The black line tunnelled me home each day and the further south we got, the hotter it seemed to be, as though we were travelling deeper down, towards the centre of the earth. The heat helped to make me dizzy and there was certainly a captive audience. Often, I let myself blur into a semi-conscious state. But so did plenty of other commuters. It wasn't much of a show. And there wasn't enough room for a back bend.

It rained a lot that summer. One evening, when I re-emerged above ground in Colliers Wood, it was raining particularly heavily. My shoes filled up with water and when I turned off the high street onto Denmark Terrace the pavement was littered with snails. They seemed to be multiplying in the warm wetness. I walked gingerly, fearing I might inadvertently crush one underfoot. I searched them out, though it was often difficult to spot their grubby tiger shells against the grubby wet stone. I nudged one with my foot, then picked it up and threw it into the air; I made it fly in a pleasing arc, so that it dropped dramatically back into the giant hydrangea in the front garden it had emerged from.

Inside number 29, Veronica was sat at the kitchen table, eating toast and poring over some papers. "You're squelching," she said, without looking up, as I came into the kitchen.

"Yes," I said. "It's raining."

Veronica looked tired but determined, as though she has been readying herself to say something to me. "I don't know where you go some nights, Ettie," she said, "and I honestly don't care. But I've got your dad breathing down my neck, and my dad, and I'm not going to let you get away with just careering off the rails." Vron crunched her toast and still didn't look at me.

I sat down. I could feel the water form a skein around my buttocks on the wooden seat and this was pleasurably distracting. The previous night, I had met Thomas again and we had gone back to the same serviced apartment. But he didn't want to talk about his family and he was on me so quick I didn't have time to hyperventilate. I knew why Vron was worried: her father is my father's brother. He's a surgeon and Vron's mother is a civil servant. As far as they are concerned, Moira was a decadent, and she'd left a dangerous legacy of potential frivolity. Veronica had clearly been tasked with trammeling me into usefulness.

"The thing is, Vron," I said, "I know what you all think. But I'm looking for something here. I am … I'm trying something."

"As a receptionist?" Vron looked up at me now with a flash of contempt; but her face softened. I imagine I looked fairly pitiful after the downpour, my hair plastered to my cheeks, my eyelashes beaded with raindrops.

I looked away from Veronica: it is hard to look at her for long without feeling entirely superfluous. Veronica is such a solid person. Her body is fed and exercised exactly to the degree that it is strong and capable, without being aesthetically distracting; her hair is cut into a bob that is practical without being self-indulgently severe; her clothes are uncoordinated, utilitarian hybrids of sports wear and work wear. Everything about Vron's appearance speaks of her practicality.

"If you want a purpose, Ettie, why don't you come and do something useful at the hospital? The phlebotomy ward is desperate for good people, and they train you on the job. If you had a skill like that, you could be *really* useful, here or anywhere else in the world." She pushed the last corner of toast into her mouth. "At least think about it, Ettie," she said, getting up. "I could take you in to shadow them one day."

"Phlebotomy?" I asked. "Isn't that blood?"

"Yes, it would mean working with blood."

"Would there be a lot of blood?"

"Well, you'd be collecting blood samples for testing. I'm sure you'd get over any queasiness. Everyone does after a while."

"Yes," I said. "The sight of blood. I'll definitely think about it."

Veronica grabbed a bag from the door. "I've got a shift," she said. "There's a leftover lasagne in the fridge."

As Veronica left, I could hear the muffled shuffle of a rodent in one of the kitchen cupboards.

That evening I lay on my bed, beneath my skylight, and thought again about the remainder of my night with Thomas. It wasn't that late when we had finished our drinks. We hadn't missed the last tube. But Thomas insisted that we go to the hotel, rather than to his flat. And his face had become over-animated when he said it. Aggressively jokey. Panicky. There was someone at home, I now concluded. Another woman. The two of us blurred together in my mind: me and whoever she might be. I lay still for a while, watching bits of glittering far-away fire in the sky through the rain-grubbed glass of the skylight. And then I had an idea. I remembered something that Maureen had said to me. "If you really want to get to know this city," Maureen had said, with a mean taunt in her voice, "you want to try online dating. You'll get the real picture there. See how much this city cares about you."

I stole downstairs and back to the kitchen. There on the table was Veronica's laptop. I huddled it to me and ran back upstairs. I started it up: no password needed. I opened the internet, typed in 'London dating' and myriad links replicated down the screen. I clicked on the first one. There were faces, immediately, head shots of grinning girls. I began to feel a slight thrill. I steadied myself, to hold it off, and began, slowly, to breathe more deeply as I explored the site.

Headshots repeated away down the left-hand side of the screen, decapitated women with glittering eyes and prehensile top-lips making strange, inviting shapes. There was also text, contained in a box next to each head. In the largest text were the pseudonyms: Just_one_dimple / Sinequanon / Geeky_Redhead / Quirky_English_Rose/ Funky_gibbon/ Lost_in_translation/ Opal74 / Piscean78/ Pepper81 / Rumi76 / Indigo_79 / Helen_of_Troy / Superwoman / ModernMarilyn / Frogkisser / Neptunia / DizzieLizzie / OneElleofagirl / ShrinkingViolet / BengalLikeTheTiger / Betterin3D / Babygurl / TinyDancer / Sunny_side / Happy_ Pepper / Smiley_spice / GoneFishing / Red_Nail_Polish / CultureVulture / CarpeDiem / HoorayForHedonism / IamMe / LastRolo / LabradorOwner.

Then, slightly smaller, came the subheaders: Do you like Bob Dylan too? / I love romping in my Hunter wellies. / I love my Vespa, cupcakes and HBO. / I like the design principles, crime series and knitwear of Scandinavia, and vitamin D. / Sunshine, tea, F. Scott Fitzgerald, 70s glass kitchenware. / Lo-fi songs are great. / Je danse, donce je suis. / What is it about France and all things French? / I love the changing seasons. / I love food. / I love all things quirky. / I really detest the smell of oranges. / I'd date me. / Not your typical Mexican gal. / Curious about Mars. / Is this what it's come to? / Write something here. / Insert subheader of your choice. / In need of subheader inspiration. / Trying to think of something smart. / Do I have to do a subheader? / ??? / Well, this is embarrassing. / I work in finance *shudder*. / I'm a divorce lawyer in the city. / I'm looking for someone who is professional. / Woof. / I'm into beards. / Call off the dogs. / You're the one for me fatty. / Don't assume. / There's no lie in her fire. / I have magnificent breasts and an adequate personality. / Mostly after your money rofl. / I'm not very good at skiing. / Who cares if the glass is half full or half empty — fill it up! / A lot of people think I look like a vegetarian lesbian, but I love meat, as much as I can fit in my mouth at one time, and more. / I want to knit you a sweater, write you a love letter. / I milked a buffalo once. / Mucho gusto. / Proceed to checkout. / I am a contradiction. / Unconventional, kind, creative. / Unconventional, witty, kind. / Unconventional, creative, down-to-earth. / I wish I had a bigger garden.

I snapped the laptop shut. The repeated, breezy, manufactured quirks I had been reading about made my head spin. I lay back and tried to enjoy it. I closed my eyes, tilted back my head. I felt for the piece of cashmere under my pillow. I let myself go a bit dreamy, feeling her approach, in the distance. I thought about making myself a profile, authoring my own iteration of detached desirability. I could try to work out a formula, an exact average of the profiles that had preceded mine. I could find the median angle of the head tilt, and the mid-point cultural reference. I could be conventionally unconventional too.

I opened my eyes and decided to take a look at the men. I zipped past writers and lawyers, environmentalists and bankers, young professionals and itinerants, filmmakers and clean-freaks, and then I spotted something of interest: a profile where the picture was not a man's head but a geometrically repeating pattern, a matrix of cubes subdivided into triangles, each concentric layer of squares dividing into more and more, smaller and smaller triangles, spiralling into a disappearing centre. When I stared at the pattern, the lighter triangles lifted out of the picture towards me, whilst the darker ones sank back, creating a 3-D tunnel effect: it looked like you could fall into it, a cut-glass mine-shaft. "I want to curate you," the header read. And then, "Artist seeks swooning beauty. Must be able to take direction. Travel to St Albans required."

VIII

Asphyxiation

I arrived at St Albans and opened the map on my phone. I walked the streets watching my own progress ghosted by the little cipher on the screen. I moved away from the centre, along wide suburban roads arboured in green. And then I reached the place where the house was meant to be. The evening was warm, but there was a soft drizzle beginning to fuzz in the air. Ahead of me, a long path led away from the road, bordered on both sides by trees. I took the path, following it as it bent sharply to the left into the grounds of a large house. The house looked as though it had once been a handsome family home; it had a red tiled roof and 1920s angles. The garden was enormous. I turned around in it. There was a big square lawn and borders full of buddleia. In the centre of the grass was a huge wooden structure, like a Maypole, with ropes extending from the top and fastened into the earth at the bottom. The garden had a freshly deserted feel to it, as though children had just been spooked into running away and their voices might trail back on the wind.

I pushed the buzzer for flat 4 and the door vibrated with a release mechanism. Inside there was a lot of post, swept to one side. Flat 1 was straight ahead and a staircase led up to the first floor. I heard a door open somewhere above me, so I took the stairs. I turned along a mezzanine landing and in the doorway to flat 4 stood a short, lean man, with curly dark hair. He had a carefully coiffed moustache and a severe strip of beard scored vertically down the centre of his chin. He held out his hand to me. "Esther," he said, looking me up and down, giving nothing away. "I'm Luke. Come in." I followed him into the flat. He was barefoot on the bare floorboards. I had guessed there might be none of the usual first-date small-talk. We turned into a large room with a fireplace. There was hardly any furniture, but positioned around the room were various exhibits. There was a chest next to the door, on top of which certain objects were meticulously laid out: a string of rosary beads, a pack of cards, a voodoo doll, a plastic leprechaun. On the mantelpiece was an animal skull, a cow's perhaps, with large flowers fixed in its empty eye-sockets, so that it looked as though the black and white chrysanthemums were blooming out of bone. In a corner there was a large glass bell-jar, filled with dead beetles. "These are some of my pieces," Luke said. "You might have seen another in the garden. That was for an open exhibition, last weekend."

"Oh, yes," I said. "The Maypole?"

"I'm thinking of burning it down," he said. "Perhaps tonight?"

"Oh," I said.

"Can I get you a drink? Perhaps some weed tea?"

"Weed tea?"

"Yes," he said, slowing his voice as if he might be dealing with an idiot. "Weed, brewed into a tea."

"Oh, right. Yes, of course. Thank you." He turned out of the room gracefully, returning after a few moments with two teacups. Fuzzy bits of green were floating on the top of the water.

"We can sit on the floor," he said. "And get to know one another."

I sipped at the tea, letting the little fronds of green enter between my teeth. I chewed on them and swallowed.

"It's a much quicker way to get high," he said, and laughed, his face lifting up in a mischievous squeeze of delight. Then he seemed to remember himself, and dropped his face back into impassivity.

"So, have you ever worked with an artist before?" he asked.

"No, not exactly," I said. I could feel a softness in my tongue and pieces of information began to loosen out of my mouth. "I'm hoping it might run in the family. My mother was a dancer and very beautiful. She posed for a lot of portraits. We have really wonderful photos of her dancing, bending all the way back and closing her eyes for the camera. And her mother was an actress. We have some early photos of her that look like paintings. They've touched up the colours, I think, when they only had black-and-white. It's so unnatural, so vivid." I was talking a lot; I was definitely getting high.

Luke was stroking his moustache. "I think we can

make something together," he said. "There's something in those eyes." He stared at my face, and then down at my body. "How are you enjoying your tea?"

The tea was making me feel strange. I was moving quickly between the desire to talk and the desire to be completely inert. He began to tell me about himself. He told me that the house was empty: the landlord was selling to developers and all the other tenants had left. But Luke was refusing to go. He'd been holding exhibitions and parties in the garden all summer long. I lay down on the floor as he spoke. I began to feel my body sinking. But small, inanimate things seemed to tick into life at the edges of my vision: the flower petals of the chrysanthemums seemed to crinkle spontaneously; the legs of the beetles seemed to flinch. Luke carried on talking. He told me about art college and that his first exhibition had been a series of oil self-portraits of himself masturbating. A comment on the contemporary art scene, he said. Saatchi had wanted to buy them, but he had refused to sell, he said, and he burnt them all at the end of the show. "I like burning things," he said. I was beginning to feel a little unnerved. I kept my eyes on him. He was playing with a lighter in his hands and he kept thumbing it to produce a spark. "Ow," he said, catching himself on the hot metal. And then he lent over towards me. "Can I kiss you, Esther?" he asked, suddenly sounding desperate. I was unsure; I began to say, "Perhaps a little later," but my lips barely moved. I probably hadn't spoken for about an hour. I had never been this stoned. I was so high I was completely dumb. Luke was attractive: his body was tight-knit with energy and there was a proud set to his small features. As he lent over, I let him kiss me with his forceful, energetic little tongue. But I was still unnerved: I was aware of the things flickering at the edges of my vision. And suddenly I felt a sharp sting against my arm. I pulled away and drew my arm towards me. There was a tiny red mark on it, in the shape of a horse shoe. It didn't hurt so much at first, but then, as I looked at it, it started to bite into my flesh. Luke was holding the lighter in his right hand. "It hurts, doesn't it?" he said, earnestly. "I wanted you to feel it too."

Then he got up and retrieved a camera from the windowsill. "Now, this is what I'd like you to do, Esther," he said. "As I said, I'm working on a project of pictures of semi-conscious people. The idea is, I'll restrict your oxygen intake, until you're just at the edge of unconsciousness. It's a wonderful feeling. It's euphoric. I know exactly where that edge is. I've done this lots of times. Here, have a look at these pictures while I get my kit." He handed over the camera, and the screen was delivering a show of various images. The first few were of Luke himself: he was laid out, naked, in front of the fireplace, in the same place that I was lying now. There was a fire in the grate behind him and a belt around his neck. In the first couple of pictures his face was puce and his body looked taut, straining against asphyxiation. In the final picture his body was relaxed, eyes closed, his head angled backwards, the top of it meeting the floorboards. Then there were pictures of girls lying naked in exactly the same position: their thin white bodies looked bleached against the bare floorboards. Some of them had the belt around their necks; some of them didn't. He'd taken close-ups of some of their faces, just before they passed out, their eyes glittering desperately. I thought I could hear a scrabbling sound, like lots of beetles skittering across the wooden floor. I thought of the empty house and the empty garden, dark now, around us. I became aware of a cloying, sweet smell in the flat. When Luke came back into the room, he was carrying a belt.

"We can do this any way you'd like," he said. "I can use the belt or I can restrict your air-flow with my hands." He squatted down beside me. And when he lent in to kiss me again, my right hand swung up into his face in a fist, smacking him hard on the side of the jaw. It knocked him backwards. I was as surprised as he was. He was temporarily dazed and then he clutched his face. "What the fuck?" he shouted. "What's wrong with you?"

I sat up, with some effort, and shook my head. I tried to rouse myself. "I'm not sure," I said. "I think it was some sort of instinct. But, please, can we still try? I think, with a few tweaks to the procedure, you'll make an excellent audience."

He got up onto his feet, rubbing at his jawline. "If you weren't comfortable, you could just have said. We went through everything beforehand, in the messages."

"I know," I said. "I think it's the tea. I thought the beetles were moving." I looked over at the glass case, still full of the brittle black bodies.

"Sleep it off," he said. "And go home in the morning."

"But we could still try?" I said.

Luke shook his head. "I'm not coming near you."

IX

Variations in Heat

A few days later, when my head had cleared, I sat behind the reception desk and thought things over. Thomas was my best opportunity, I thought. Maureen eyed me suspiciously, as though she knew I was up to something. It was still raining; people drove the revolving doors open, clutching soggy newspapers over their heads, their suits drenched a darker shade of grey around the silhouettes of their makeshift rain shelters.

At the end of the day, I decided to walk up to Hampstead Heath. It was a short uphill burst in the drizzle, past large Art Deco blocks of flats and then enormous, gated white houses. When I reached the matrix of tightly turning streets that make up the centre, I wandered around them, looking for the coffee shop that might be Thomas's. There were lots of beautiful old houses converted into shops, displaying expensive copper kitchenware in their brightly lit windows. There were mannequins draped in this season's brights. There were windows full of glowing blue bottles, filled with organic beauty potions. The smell of mandarin blossom trailed me down the street. I crossed the main road and took a set of stone steps, which wound steeply upwards between terraced houses in a ginnel. It was almost like a Pennine village. But at the very top there was a break in the buildings and I could suddenly see all the way across London: the knobbled BT tower was in the foreground; and then, softly fuzzed in the peach sky behind it stood the wheel; other buildings towered up in the distance, where the orangey-pink sky fogged into grey, like the flesh of cooked salmon darkening at the edges. I carried on walking: small pubs were hidden away up here, already full of gregarious after-work drinkers. I found myself at the top of Hampstead and snaked back down. Finally, in a narrow passage off the main hub of streets, I peered into a coffee-shop window. The sign on the door said 'Closed'. There was a man at the counter, with his back turned to the window, a tea-towel wrapped around one of his hands. He was disengaging nozzles from a coffee machine and then rinsing them in the sink. After a few moments he turned around: it was Thomas. At that moment a woman, who had been sat unnoticed by me at one of the tables, stood up and moved to meet him. They embraced. Thomas's hands were in the woman's hair and he was pulling her in towards him. Watching this felt oddly thrilling; I was ghosting the woman, several feet behind her. I was mesmerised by their kissing. Then they disentangled. I ducked around the side of the window, into a recessed doorway. I waited a few moments, my heart beating hard. And then the woman banged the coffee-shop door open and walked quickly away. My legs moved me rapidly after her, across the street and back down the hill. The momentum in my body was exciting. The two of us were now moving in series back down the high street towards Swiss Cottage. The woman walked so quickly that I felt like I was tumbling after her. When we got down to Avenue Road, the woman made a sharp right, and my feet automatically followed. She diverted into the big, grey, cubed complex of the leisure centre, and I found myself behind her at the barriers; then I was watching her back disappearing through another set of doors.

"I'm sorry," said the woman on the kiosk. "Helen's class is fully booked this evening."

"Helen's class?" I turned to the woman.

"Yes, Helen's hot yoga," the woman inclined her head towards the cooling trail. "I can book you in for her class tomorrow evening though," she offered.

"Oh, yes, please," I said.

When I entered the room, the heat hit me like a solid force. And then there was the smell: people were already sweating and the salty musk was rising, adding to the force of the hot air. One man, stood just in speedos, had already dripped a raggedy silhouette of himself onto his mat, light purple shading into dark around his body. I picked a spot towards the back of the room and laid out the mat I'd borrowed from the centre. It had faded to a dusty pink through use and I could smell the fusty accumulations of feet and sweating backs that had gone before me. I lay down on it and breathed deeply. The lights were dimmed and Helen entered the room, picking her way through the group to the front. She held herself beautifully, chin tilted slightly upwards, limbs fully articulated, as though her whole body was perfectly choreographed from her navel. She moved like a dancer, and her thick bob swung against her cheeks with each step. She placed tiny plastic candles in front of her mat, which flickered with a battery-powered flame, and then she struck a tiny cymbal.

"The mat is bread, your body is butter," she intoned flatly. "Melt your body into the mat."

After a cycle of nostril breathing, during which I tried hard not to succumb to the temptation to pass out, Helen talked the class through sun salutations. "*Listen* to my instructions," she insisted. "Don't look at the people around you. They're probably doing it wrong." I followed the directions and moved my body through a sequence of bends and lunges and genuflections. The heat was really something; everyone was sweating freely now and the odour seemed to expand in the space. "If you're new, lie down if you need to," Helen said. "The body needs to adjust to the heat. But you. Must. Not. Leave. The room. Sudden temperature drop is *extremely* detrimental." Helen patrolled the rows as she barked out the next position: downward dog. I pushed my weight backwards, lifting my body into the triangular inversion. Helen approached down the row, and when she reached me she put her hands on the base of my back, pushing me further backwards. The pressure

Helen exerted against my body was tender but disinterested. "Spread your hands flat," Helen said. "They should be flat against the floor." She pushed me a little harder, so that my face moved closer to the mat, and then she moved off to adjust someone else. All this was making me feel light-headed: if I looked to the right I could see all of us in the mirrored wall, our various repeated inverted-v postures. Our bodies echoed one another's. When I stood up, there was a slight swimming at the corners of my eyes, and the heat pushed itself more fiercely around and into my body. It was almost too much to bear. I began to move towards a backbend. "Do *not* close your eyes." Helen was right in front of me. Her voice was followed by an aggressive waft of patchouli. "You'll lose balance. *Awareness* in the room please." I had to open my eyes. This banished the beautiful blurring. In fact, I suddenly felt fantastically clear-headed, as though my consciousness was beating against the heat more strongly. My body moved easily through the postures, the warmth seeming to open my joints into fluidity. Helen continued with her firm instructions as she paced down the rows. As the postures got more advanced, she commanded the class more sternly. "If you do not follow my instructions exactly, you will INJURE YOUR NECK," she barked. She talked us through a headstand. "Everyone can do this, if you just follow my instructions," she said. "I don't understand why *some people* can't just follow instructions." And then she reeled around and pointed at an overweight woman on the front row. "Except you. You can't do this. Lie on your back."

At the end of the session we all lay back down on our mats. I thought again about the layering of bodies, all of us laid out now in series, and all the other bodies who had left their traces on my mat. I began to let myself go. But as Helen ordered us all to melt into our mats, the angry little catch in her voice kept drawing me back out. It wasn't going to work. When I flickered my eyes open, I saw Helen standing by the mirrors at the front, stretching and admiring her own angles.

The sky was still light when I emerged from the sports centre. I had showered there, scrubbing hard at my face while I thought about Helen and Thomas. The scenario felt less promising now. I needed to work out what I could try next. I took the Tube to Waterloo and decided to head above ground. I walked towards the river, intending to walk home as far as I could along it. On the South Bank there were flamenco dancers and children screaming on a giant trampoline. The sun was just about to sink below the buildings on the opposite bank, and it seemed to glow blindingly bright in its final moments. My skin still felt raw. I imagined it accumulating the dirt from around me, taking everything in. I kept on walking. I passed grand cast-iron lamp-posts decorated with huge scaley fish that seemed to regurgitate the lamp-posts like a synchronised magic trick.

I passed the Houses of Parliament, its dark patterned surface like a gothic wedding cake. As the towers of Battersea Power Station appeared intermittently on the horizon, the streetlights became fluorescent strips and the other pedestrians thinned out. There was a man sitting on a bench up ahead, who was talking animatedly. There didn't seem to be anybody material that he was talking to; I assumed he must be using a phone earpiece. The man was wearing a cheap green anorak and, as I drew alongside him, I could see a polyester skirt, a blouse and pair of shoes laid out next to him on the bench. He had dressed the empty silhouette of a woman. He continued to speak animatedly to the clothes as I passed.

I carried on walking until the path at the side of the Thames disappeared into riverside apartments and the sky had become a grey-violet haze. Then I was forced into Vauxhall and drifted until I found the Tube.

Later, deep into the night, I woke. I lay in the thick black and thought of Veronica asleep in the room below me; and then of the hundreds of people nestled in sleep along our street. And I thought of all the other streets of Colliers Wood, full of sleeping people, sleeping people I would never know, and who would never know me. I lay there in my cocoon of dark, a secret to them, to all the unmourning strangers of London. We were mirroring one another in our poses of unconsciousness.

And we were all composed of the same thing. What would it be like to see it, to see this thing we all shared? I clicked back my skylight blind, to let in the starlight. I watched the winking planes circle low and wide over the city, like a night-time vigil over all our dark bodies. My breathing slowed and I was folded back into sleep.

X

The Sight of Blood

St George's Hospital was sheened linoleum as far as the eye could see. Which was not very far: vision was limited to low-ceilinged corridors, cut off by sharp corners. I followed the signs for Phlebotomy, which took me out of the main building, across two car parks, and then into a squat '60s prefab. I introduced myself at the desk.

"Oh, yeah, the work experience girl," said a tired-looking woman in a thin blue pyjama suit.

"Well, not exactly," I said. "I —"

The woman picked up the phone and called through to someone. "A Freestone here for you." After a few moments, a young, extremely plump woman wearing green overalls bustled into the waiting room.

"You must be Esther," she said kindly, without breaking her walk, encouraging me to trot alongside her down a corridor and into an examination room. "I'm Carmilla. I've heard such a lot about you from Veronica. She's so pleased you're coming in." The woman motioned for me to take a seat on one of the plastic chairs. "So," Carmilla wound a strand of blonde hair behind her ear and looked over a clipboard. "We'll be seeing lots of different people today for lots of different tests. You'll get a good sense of the range of patients we deal with." Carmilla's voice was soft and refined; the walking had made her slightly breathless, so she sounded like an aristocratic coquette. "Some of them are regulars. Others might never have had a blood test before." She looked at her watch. "We've got a few minutes, so I can go over the equipment." Carmilla got out several small drawers full of plastic-wrapped apparatus. "Ok, this is what we use most commonly," she said, still slightly breathless, "for a straightforward venopuncture, when we want to draw blood from here." Carmilla turned her own arm tender-side up and rolled back the long-sleeved top she was wearing under her overalls. She flexed her elbow and massaged the braced nook. "So, you can't see much at the moment, but the cubital fossa, anterior to the elbow, is the best place to draw blood: the median cubital vein is close to the surface and has minimal nerve supply." I watched Carmilla continue to work the patch of flesh: at first I could only see the tiny dark-blue threads close to the surface of Carmilla's skin, so delicate they looked like penned lines; but then, in the centre of the articulated fold, a vein began to rise into a small greenish bulge.

"So, on this kind of vein we'd usually go for a vacuum tube." Carmilla rolled her sleeve back down and shook one of the plastic packets. "You'll see a lot of these today. We use one hypodermic needle and multiple vacuum tubes can be attached if we need to take multiple samples." Carmilla tossed the packet back in a drawer. "You can use a fingerstick for small tests. Or, if you were dealing with a very small baby, a neonatal heelstick. Do you want tea and a biscuit? You look a little bit pale, my darling." Carmilla placed her hand on my arm and gave it a firm squeeze. "You're not squeamish are you, you lovely thing? We haven't even seen any blood yet!" She bustled out of the room, her overalls rustling like paper.

I stared at the lucent floor tiling; it had been polished until the plastic looked like solid liquid. It was unsettling to see Carmilla's vein beneath the surface of her skin: the little rising glut of blue-green, a tiny glimpse of the obscene territory underneath. I felt a swirl in my stomach at the thought of the blood to come, as though my own internal material was clustering in readiness to meet it.

Carmilla pushed the door open with her behind, and re-entered the room with two plastic cups of tea, biscuits stacked up high on top of one another. She cooed over me for a while, making me drink the sugary tea, and then she talked me through the different tubes that are used in different blood tests: some came ready-prepared with additives to prevent the blood from clotting; others, for tests where clotting time was at stake, contained citrates; some were laced with clotting accelerators. It would be my job today to hand over the correct tubes, under Carmilla's instruction. The first patient was a regular, Carmilla explained: a heavily pregnant woman who was rhesus negative. She was being tested regularly because her baby was at risk of erythroblastosis fetalis: to put it simply, Carmilla said, the mother's antibodies might travel through the placenta and attack the red blood cells in foetal circulation, the blood cells that the baby needed. "The mother and baby's blood is a shared system, but sometimes it turns nasty," Carmilla said, with a deliciously naughty inflection.

Carmilla buzzed through to reception and, a few moments later, there was a knock at the door. The pregnant woman pushed her way in and sat down heavily on a chair.

"How are you today, Ruth?" Carmilla asked.

"Tired," said the woman. "Work keep breathing down my neck; coming in late after all these tests."

"Right, well let's get on with it then. Left today." Carmilla pulled on latex gloves and directed me towards the correct tube; then she fixed it to the gleaming hypodermic. She stepped over towards the woman, who had already pulled up her sleeve and was looking away, uninterested, towards the door. Carmilla palpated the stretched crux of the woman's arm, gently, tenderly, as she had done her own: and sure enough, a bluer vein began to rise up. She took the needle to the most acute angle and eased it gently into the skin, so that the moment of incision was impossible to detect. And then the tube began to fill. The colour of the blood in the light blue room was incredible; it bloomed upwards, a lurid and gorgeous coagulation. I was drawn towards it. I couldn't help it. I started to hyperventilate, so subtly that they couldn't have heard. The woman's face flickered as the needle retracted. But otherwise, once Carmilla had whipped the tube away, it seemed inconceivable that the woman was made of blood: that, underneath her floral maxi-dress and smooth skin, a complex network of gore was developing inside her; that between the matted placenta and the gathering body of the new baby, a potentially treacherous blood ecology was evolving. I remembered the word *exsanguinated* and felt my pulse tick in my lips and my cheeks. I let my head fall backwards a little and closed my eyes. "Esther, darling, are you ok?" Carmilla clamped a hand on my shoulder.

"Oh, I'm fine," I said and brought my head upright. Carmilla was too vigilant; I'd never get away with any kind of performance.

Not all the patients were as straightforward to bleed as the first. There was an elderly woman later in the morning, whose veins looked as though they were tougher than any other patient's: they rose up through the skin of her arms, fat and solidly blue, as soon as she clenched her fist. But apparently her veins were collapsing. She was a regular too. Carmilla asked me to find her a butterfly needle and tried a new approach, glinting towards a tiny new vein that she thought might be branching off the collapsing course. The woman's arm was so thin that there was nothing plump to rest the point of the needle against; the insertion looked more like a blind stab. And it didn't work the first time. The blood clotted too quickly and stopped being drawn up the tube. The old woman leaned her head back and groaned. Her arm dangled limply and was yellowed all over in bruise-blotches. I looked for the branching veins, the new tributaries splitting off where the old had failed. I remembered something from school: that blood vessels are fractal, repeating their self-similar shapes over and over, darkly branching under the skin again and again and again. Finally, Carmilla extracted a sample she could use, and the woman hugged her rain mac back around her, as if to protect herself from further violence.

Our final patient of the morning blundered into the room and came to a halt right in front of us, drawing himself up. His body was strange: he held himself tall, barrelling out his chest, as though squaring up for a fight, but his arms hung limp from his torso. I realised he must be drunk, because of the smell. And then I saw that he was already bleeding: there was blood spattered down his bare right leg, blackening on the fabric of his shorts. This was no longer as odd as it would have been a few hours ago, in the outside world; no longer obscene, the blood was merely in the wrong place. I followed the red line upwards and saw that the end of the man's middle finger was raggedy; no solid curve of skin, just a fray of blood.

"Mr Stevens, Jack, isn't it?" Carmilla was up on her feet, deftly steering the man into a chair. "You're bleeding already, my darling. I'm just going to call someone to see to that." She picked up her phone and requested an auxiliary to dress a wound. "Now then, Jack, you need to tell us what happened to your finger."

The man extended his leg, rigid, so his body formed a hard hypotenuse. "Can't remember, can I?" he said and swept his arm across his sweating face. "Woke up in the shed. And then I was rushing to get here. Late. Must've caught it on something." He had left a smudge of blood across his forehead and now his finger was dripping onto the linoleum. A knock at the door and then a woman with a plastic case came in. She smiled kindly at the man and he held his hand out like a child towards her: he seemed almost proud of the strange finger. The woman cleaned it and dressed it into an enormous white bulb. "Ha!" said the man. Another woman came into the room to clean and disinfect the floor.

"Can nurse get you something for the pain?" Carmilla asked.

"Can't feel a thing," the man responded, turning over his bandaged hand again and again.

Carmilla took blood from his other arm. He barely seemed to notice. "You need to take care of yourself, Jack," she said.

"No one to care if I take care of myself or not," he said, cheerfully.

"Results will come to your doctor," Carmilla said, showing him out. And then she turned back to me. "Now

then, you've got the blood in your cheeks back, young lady,"
she said.

"Oh, yes, I'm absolutely fine," I said. "But it was still
very interesting."

Veronica met me outside the entrance to A&E. She was wearing
green pyjamas and her thick hair was pulled back into a tiny
hard stub of ponytail.

"So, how was it?" she asked as we walked together
through the car park. "You didn't freak out, did you?"

"No, not exactly," I said. "I thought it was pretty
amazing." It was drizzling warmly again, gauzing over the
road in front of us.

"Right," said Veronica. "So shall we look into
phlebotomy training for you?"

"Oh no," I said. "I mean, I wouldn't be very good for
the patients. I'd get totally lost in it."

Veronica turned her face skywards and raised her
palms in a gesture of frustration. "I don't understand you,
Ettie. Don't you want to do anything useful at all?"

"I don't know," I said. "I'm just trying to... There's
something, first, I still need to try to —"

Veronica's phone rang from behind her, inside the
small burgundy rucksack she wore across one shoulder. She
shrugged the bag off and dug out the phone.

"Hello?" She listened for a moment and then passed the phone across to me. "It's your father. He's being dramatic."

XI
The Flood

As the train pulled out of King's Cross, a woman with bright yellow hair pushed a trolley amiably down the aisle, calling out "sandwiches and coffee" in a market cadence. It rained all the way up to Leeds; and then it rained all the way across to Todmorden. Blue and brown fields streamed past the train.

"We have a rainy season now," one old man on the train was saying to another. I couldn't see their faces, but their words came out in long, low rumbles, with great pauses in between. "Just. Like. India."

The water on the window was collecting in multiplying beads. The beads seemed entirely still, until they suddenly merged and streamed away down the outside pane.

"It's global. Warming."

Field upon field of cabbages blurred past through the water, glimmering blue lakes of greens.

"Then why. Aren't. We any. Warmer?"

As we pulled into the valley, I could see that the fields either side of the canal were covered in still brown water. The whole valley bottom looked brown.

"You know. It's the Gulf. Stream. Being affected."

What was strange was the stillness of the water. It was as though it had always covered these areas, as though the playing fields had never existed. The green had disappeared without a trace.

"I *don't*. Know."

My father picked me up from the train station in his truck. When we got to the bottom road, where the street crosses the river, brown surface water covered the tarmac and all the gutters were gushing. Cars drove slowly, kicking up water around them.

"This is much better!" my father said. "Yesterday it was practically impassable. And further down it was completely flooded. Waist deep. We were cut off for the whole day. We've had reports of cars stranded, people wading to safety up at Morrisons. All sorts of things. We're running a story on an elderly woman living between the canal and the river. The water flooded her house a couple of nights ago, and she was trapped upstairs with her miniature poodle for 12 hours. Nobody could get near her. Five feet of it, pouring from the river into the canal through her house. She spent most of the night talking on the phone to my reporter."

We turned off the main road and drove over the bridge to the house. We pulled up. There was very little surface water left here but there was a residual brown soddenness to everything. The garden looked like it had leaked slurry, filthy wetness swelling up out of the ground and spreading in all directions.

Inside the house, the smell was terrible: salty, sludgy damp. There was still an oily film of water covering the carpets.

"Look what the council helpfully dropped off." Dad motioned towards a box on the kitchen table. "Tins of spam and sandbags."

I took my things upstairs. The bedrooms hadn't got wet, but the electricity was off, so everything felt even more dismal than usual. I changed my clothes and quickly checked on her room. Everything had remained the same. I spent the next few hours helping Dad to sort through his effects, separating the recoverable from the terminally sodden. Then we started to move things upstairs or outside, so that he could take up the wet carpets. There was a constant anxious whirr in the background: the sound of the pump pulsing water out of the cellar. I surprised a frog in the sideboard and there were weird black molluscs clinging to the skirting boards.

I was down on my hands and knees, forcing more water up out of carpet around me, when I found it. I was sorting through some things in the bottom of the dresser, to see whether the water had got to them. It was mostly full of boxes of records, which felt a little damp but seemed like they might recover. Between these boxes I found an old tin, embossed in gold, with an Art Nouveau woman iconised on the lid. The tin seemed to spring open in my hands and it was full of small, beautiful things. A ring, a glittering brooch, a little cut-glass cube. I picked the last object up. It was familiar. It looked a bit like a squat salt shaker, full of white powder, but instead of perforations on the top, there was a battered silver screw-cap. It had lived on her drinks cabinet, that's where I recognised it from: it was one of Moira's curiosities. I was holding it up as Dad walked into the room. He froze on the threshold when he saw what was in my hands.

"Put that box down, please, Esther," he said, after a moment.

"What is this?" I said, turning the cube up to the light.

"It's ... it's something your mother inherited. From her mother." He stepped towards me. "Smelling salts. Salt of hartshorn. Made from the ground-up antlers of deer, allegedly. It'd burn out your mucus membranes if you weren't careful." He was being suspiciously jovial with his voice now, but his eyes had gone small, narrowed with concentration. "It was supposed to stop you from fainting. And your grandmother was a fine one for pretending she was always about to faint. An actress, as you know." He placed one hand on my shoulder. "Let's put these old things away," he said, reaching out towards the tin.

It was then that I spotted it: slantways between the glittering glass and dull metal stood a violet envelope. I snatched it out of the tin. The words "Vincent and Esther" were curled across the front of the envelope in my mother's writing.

"And what's this?" I asked him.

My father let his hand fall away from me and he staggered backwards. "Don't touch it," he said. "Please, put it away." He had come to rest against the wall. "I can't," he said, "I can't look at these things any more. I can't think about her anymore." He was crumpled and pink-cheeked, sliding slowly towards the floor.

I needed to see what was in the envelope. Its tongue had been folded tightly back into its mouth and the paper rasped as I opened it. It was a note, written in my mother's over-elaborate hand. It began without preamble:

> *Dearest Vincent, You trapped me here, in this specially constructed glass case. Perhaps this is what you always wanted? I shall die so beautifully you will never forget it. Open casket please.*

Then there was a small dividing line, scored across the middle of the page.

> *Dearest Esther, It feels like the ocean and I cannot resist it. Give your audience something they will always remember.*

And that was it. The words ended there. No affectionate sign-off, no little cross kisses. I stared across at my father. He was still squatting awkwardly against the wall, his face averted. I read the two paragraphs again. "What does it mean?"

My father glanced up at me, paused, seeming to weigh up his options. "Your mother was very ill, at the end," he said. "Delusions of grandeur. Paranoia. Most of all drunk. But it was still a twisted thing to do."

"So she wrote this just before she died? That means she knew she was about to die?"

He carried on looking at me, a spasm of mirth twitching at the corners of his mouth. "Yes, Esther, she knew. And you're supposed to be a bright girl. I thought you might have worked it out by now. She *did it*. By her own hand, as they say. She took the drugs, she posed her body like that, and then she waited."

I looked at the letter again but I couldn't seem to read it. "So, you're saying she was at peace? She knew she was going to die, and that's why she … wrote this?" I asked.

"Not at peace, for god's sake, not that. She took matters into her own hands. Listen to me. She refused treatment and then she did it."

She had looked so beautiful when I found her. And when I raised the alarm that day, crying like a baby gull, my father had come up after me. He'd ushered me out of the room and the whole process had been set in motion. They'd taken her away, they'd boxed her up, they'd buried her. I didn't see her again. But I knew that we'd both seen her like that, her body finalised in that perfect arch. I thought we'd both kept that scene safe, that we'd both cherished how serene she looked.

"Do you think anyone looks that perfect, when they die, really, Ettie? They don't. They look ghastly. They look exhausted and emptied out. No, it was her vanity. She wanted to produce a final, devastating performance. She choreographed the whole thing." My father slid down to the soggy floor and let his head drop dramatically.

I was part of her audience, then, that was all; I'd always been part of her disappointingly small audience. I looked around the room, at the dingy wetness, at my father's heaving body. If I shut my eyes right now I knew I could do it — I'd be able to feel her flicker inside me, I'd be able to shut straight down. But I didn't do it. I held my eyes right open and I widened them as far as I could, straining to take it all in.

I walked out of the house, heading over the bridge and into town. The water was flowing in the usually-still canal and looked close to spilling over. I walked onto the main road, past the giant Portakabin that houses the Aldi. A woman in green overalls was sweeping water out of the front door. I kept along the main road: all the shops were closed and people inside were sweeping their floors, the tell-tale brown tide-marks making dirty ripples along white walls. There were mounds of sodden carpet periodically blocking the pavement. The bad green sludge smell followed me everywhere.

The graveyard wasn't flooded, though the ground was boggy. The parkland next to the church is part of the flood-defence system, so the river had been diverted into it. It was now one enormous brown pool, with a red climbing frame rising up from its centre. I walked between the graves. The Murgatroyd house stood blackly ahead, interposing itself between the A646 and the buried. There were some boys over in the corner of the graveyard nearest the woods, sitting on the wall, wearing their hoods pulled up and smoking reefers. I could smell the greenness of the skunk through the damp air. I kept up my slow procession until I found the grave. There were tiny goldfinches darting around in the trees above it, like fluttering leaves. I lay down to watch them and I could feel the back of my head beginning to get cold, the damp soaking into my hair and seeping around the skin on my skull. I could hear the boys laughing and I thought of the dried plants burning to orange in their fingers and then moving with their breath into their lungs. I thought about the fractal branching of their bronchioles, the tiny vessels splitting again and again, filling up with hot smoke. And then I thought of the woods behind them, each tree forking out its branches, spitting out self-replicating adjuncts of wood, over and over. Each tree tells you how many trees there are in the surrounding wood, through the pattern of its twigs: that was Mr Nield from geography again. If the forest is one big algorithm, then it is full of wooden self-replicators, zombie trees. I closed my eyes and thought of all the water around us, coursing down the sides of streets, rippling across the over-full grates, seeping downwards into the soil, watering all the tiny organisms feasting deep inside the earth. If I concentrated, I could hear the water gurgling over the bubbling sounds of the boys' voices. If I lay here long enough, perhaps I would begin to break down, to be reconstituted as sodden ground. I imagined my skin, the thick pad of it, full of parasites, softening into earth. I thought about all of our bodies: mother's and mine; the boys and their lungs; the trees and their branches. My body was beginning to do it. Force of habit. My breathing was speeding up, ready to shut down.

But I wouldn't do it, I wouldn't pass out. I remembered that little bottle, the hartshorn. I thought of the burning sensation that might force you upright. I imagined myself as a sting, a graze against the surface of the world around me, and I opened my eyes.

An old woman with white hair and a large rain hat was leaning over me. "Are you able to stand?" she asked, sharply.

"Yes, don't worry. I was just —"

"Well then, get to your feet, young lady," the woman said. "There's an awful lot to do."

The woman walked briskly away down the path and then turned back towards me, summoning me up. I got to my feet. The back of my body was cold with damp. I wondered if I was marked, a line dividing me between dry and wet like a jester suit, cut halfway between the living and the dead.

The woman was kneeling on a muddy cushion in front of a flower bed, and she drew a trowel from an old basket. She turned back towards me again. "Well, are you helping or are you hindering?" I moved closer to her. "Now then," she said. "These are waterlogged. We need to make courses around the roots of each plant, so that the water can drain, and then we're going to add some sand to the soil." The woman continued to look at me, studying me for further signs of derangement. "You can do the sand," she said, handing me a heavy bag of orange mixture.

I crouched beside her and followed the lines of her trowel, sprinkling the sand in circles around each plant's roots.

"I planted all of these, you know," the woman said. "A group of us do it. Guerilla gardeners. Wherever there's unused land, we've planted it. We've done legumes in front of the police station, and fruit trees in the supermarket borders, and herbs around the health centre. Now I'm cultivating from the dead." She hummed a little tune, and then she turned on me with her glossy, goitrous blue eyes. "And why are you falling down in graveyards, young lady?"

I stared at the ground and continued to pour out the sand.

The woman carried on scooping away at the earth and said nothing for a while. Then, "Do you know, we share 35 per cent of our genetic coding with daffodils? Did you know that? Daffodils are extremely beautiful. And they stand up," the woman said.

"Yes," I said, and I thought of the daffodils that spring up each year in that graveyard, rising from the dead, nosing their way upright through the earth, repeating themselves upwards over and over from their onion skins, and then flinching brightly in the breeze.

"They say I have cancer, you know," the woman said. "Of course you don't know. It makes no difference. It's growing, slowly, every day. They say I'll die *with* it, not *of* it. I'll be brought in here one of these days and I still make the effort to get up. You don't just lie down about these things." The woman knelt up with her back straight and turned her attention to the raspberry bushes.

I continued to pour the sand in careful, repeated circles. I thought of the cancer growing inside this woman next to me, its cells reproducing through her organs in beautifully exact patterns, like snowflakes. I pushed my shoulders back and felt upwards into my height. I felt a bloom of fresh blood through my abdomen, where a vessel was opening up. There was a pulse there, a deep flicker inside me. I doubled the old woman now: slowly, carefully, I shadowed the woman's movements in sand as the rain began, again, to fall.